D0730610

For Ardean, Loretta, and Irene
Three very different women, three beautiful stories
And three strong sets of shoulders that I stand upon

"For all that we encounter, is all we must accept."

PROLOGUE: OLIVIA, SIXTY YEARS OLD (TWENTY-EIGHT YEARS AGO)

"Shalom," I whisper.

It's a good start, but it must be perfect.

I say it again, slower, emphasizing the syllables and extending the "om." It's soothing, benevolent, but it's obvious and impersonal. It needs more. I've traveled this far. There should be no confusion about what I seek: for me, for him, and yes, perhaps most importantly, for her. Decisively, I write:

Shalom. Bring peace to those I've loved, and please, bring peace to me.

Respectfully,

Olivia

The ink of the felt tip marker bleeds through. For good measure, I underline "please," then bow in reverence, to whom or what I do not know. But in this place, surrounded by the faithful, it feels appropriate. I have nothing to lose. Anything of value to me has already been taken.

I stand before the Western Wall. Prayers burst at the seams, crammed and flared like fans from limestone blocks. The wall is forty-five layers of stone in all, twenty-eight of which loom above ground, kissing the sky at a dizzying sixty-two feet. Toward the top, beyond reach for hands to prune, puffs of weeds sneak between rows. Mini, dried-out oases that thirst for water but, like heads in a pillory, are trapped in a patchwork of beige and brown, subjected to the harsh, Israeli sun.

"Olivia!" Jeffrey taps his watch, the signal to re-collect. The others gather, but it's only half the group. I have time.

At six-foot-one and a buck fifty, his gangly stride is exaggerated by a slightly pigeon-toed gate that with each step teeters the bifocals on his beak-like nose. He's a high-strung history buff better suited for an academic classroom than a guided tour.

I cup my ear, pretending not to hear. "What?" I mouth coyly.

Before he can elaborate, Milton's tapping his shoulder. An opportune distraction. A foot shorter, Milton's hot breath radiates off Jeffrey's chin. His pen furiously scribbling details on a notepad that'll later line his scrapbook page.

"She's better off finding a four-leaf clover," quips Clara, a beautician from Connecticut. She leans against Gerry, her husband, with acrylic nails covering red stained lips. It's a snide remark fitting to the culprit. She's centered herself in the group, which I've found is her nature, always gravitating to where the spotlight shines.

"Enough, Clar." Gerry swats her hand, no patience for gossip.

Her jaw drops, appalled. "Don't be daft," she snaps. "Her little wish is delaying our dinner."

But she can wait. With hope, or spite, I crisply fold the paper to a quarter's size and find a crack to fill. Chalky sediment clings to my dewy fingers like talcum powder, leaving a dusty film. I step back, pleased, or at least satisfied, with my contribution. And yet, Clara's words have done their damage. I'm sardined among a crowd of worshipers fighting for my prayer to be heard, and after assessing the competition, mine hasn't a shot in hell.

Their wails are haunting. Heaved from bellies with strained desperation that summon veins to their surface. A frail, elderly woman boasts the loudest cry, her scalp enveloped in a midnight blue shpitzel. Not a strand of hair peeks through. Her curved spine projects a foghorn voice, rattling off Yiddish and taking advantage of the plaza's acoustics, bulldozing her well-versed tkhine past contenders for ethereal ears. "Have mercy!" she begs, deeply invested in her daughter's fertility.

"There, you see it?" Jeffrey's tilted back, bent at the waist with hands on hips. A star, Sirius, ascends in the southeast corner of a pinched-pink sky. The first of the night. His lean arm directs Milton's gaze, who looks up, briefly, then returns to his notes, asking if an *i* or *e* follows the s. The thickening atmosphere becomes a prism, the magic hour when the world's quixotic lighting turns man-made structures into natural wonders. An intangible stopwatch starts: eighteen minutes left of twilight. The energy heightens in preparation for Shabbat.

The crowd swarms in clusters dense as twenty. Claustrophobia kicks in.

Jeffrey starts to fidget, rubbernecking between heads. "Three, four, five," he counts, sharply stabbing the air as each number's called. We're easy to spot, an eyesore of shoulder-padded blouses and Calvin Klein jeans brought from the States. Slowly, I inch toward the group. All around us, whispers weave between jutted chins and hunched shoulders, carried by the dense, moist air.

"OK, let's go!" He uses his rainbow umbrella like a shepherd's staff, guiding his flock to the air-conditioned bus. Long faces sluggishly convene.

"Also known as the Wailing Wall, Kotel, or Al-Buraq, it was in this spot where..." Now with breathing room, Jeffrey resumes his duties and relays historical facts. "The first temple was built by King Solomon, son of David; destroyed twice, first by the Babylonians, and next by the Romans; Jewish tradition foretells that a third and final temple will be built, making it the holiest site in Judaism, and the point of reference during prayer; for Sunni Muslims, it is the location of Muhammad's ascent to heaven, and home to al-Aqsa Mosque and Dome of the Rock..."

Having done my homework, I amble in the rear.

"Hey, Olivia," a wheezy voice whispers. It's Milton, whose ballpoint pen now kneads the doughy fat of my back.

"What?" I step forward, annoyed with the behavior and its perpetrator.

Two bubbled eyes flinch behind thick lenses, unprepared for my sharp reply, one *much* less congenial than Jeffrey's. But unlike Jeffrey, I'm not paid to entertain his inquiries.

"I was wondering..." The spiral notepad shields his chest, bursting with battered bookmarks and Post-its. "Well, you seemed so, so dedicated earlier, by the wall, and well, I..."

"*What,* Milton?"

His posture straightens, faking confidence. "Well, what did you wish for?"

"Ex-*cuse* me?"

He tends to an inner nostril itch, nose pointed to the sky and anchored with lightly pursed lips. He's clueless to the intimacy of the question. Even a child knows not to ask the birthday celebrant their wish before blowing out the candle. It's bad luck.

"How is that any of your business?"

But Milton carries an innocence that's oddly endearing, with eyebrows that flick back and forth like flippers on a pinball machine, awaiting answers as if they're shiny silver balls rolling down the ramp. Gullibly, I cave.

"If you must know, I wished for a sort of reassurance."

"Reassurance?"

"Yes. A sign, or a feeling. Anything, really. Reassurance that it was worth it. That it served a purpose, and most importantly, that there are better days to come. I'd like to know there's hope for me yet."

"But aren't you in your sixties?"

"Yes, *Milton*, but I'm not dead."

He mulls it over until a hard blink signifies that he accepts the possibility I still have valuable years to live.

"So then, *what* exactly served a purpose?"

"The *pain,* Milton." I pop the "*pay* for emphasis. If said correctly, with just enough asperity, it should shut him up. If he was expecting a luxury sedan with all the bells and whistles, he asked the wrong girl. I don't owe him my life story.

Thankfully, the tactic works. Color drains from his cheeks, and I'm pleased. After a quick nod, his tiny stride takes off to reclaim his role as Jeffrey's shadow.

What I don't bother to say, is that what he understood to be "dedication" was in fact *desperation*. The Western Wall is my last trip. I'm tired. All of these years, though I stood alone when soliciting my wish, I came on the behalf of those who could not be with me. Those I've loved. Those whose pain is the root of my own.

But even if Milton dared to continue, the time for questions has run out.

Soon, we're swallowed by bodies.

The men march in unison with white kippahs shielding their skulls, while women gather in ensembles removed from their male counterparts. A partition separates the sexes like the splitting of the Red Sea. They sing words I've studied, in a language I failed miserably to master, with voices of hope, desperation, sadness, praise; heralding the Shabbat queen, "*Tzeitchem l'shalom Mal'achei Hashalom...*"

Each limb cloaked in fabric, barely a pore exposed. They're unbothered, accustomed to the suffocating heat, while I cook like a rotisserie chicken. Sweat soaks the linen scarf wrapping my neck and mouth, used to filter the stench. Losing stamina, I inhale, and realize the biggest offender is me.

Feeling faint, I stumble back and gasp for air, seeking a pocket of space. There's no relief. My pace quickens through the crowd and toward the gate, fighting the oncoming traffic of bodies. Colors, shapes, sounds blur into one confounded mass, until the floor shifts beneath my feet, and then...*smack*. Darkness.

"*As-salāmu ʿalaykum*," a meek, young voice calls. He speaks Arabic.

Dirt cakes my jeans. A bump swells where my cheek hit stone. Embarrassed, I readjust the mat I've stumbled over. I must keep going. Jerusalem has its share of street merchants, highly skilled vendors with a polished sales pitch, but I have no money. I'll appear rude if I'm unable to respond, and hand gestures paint me as a disrespectful American, unwilling to learn the basics of her host country's language.

"Miss! Miss! Excuse me!" he speaks again, this time in English. "Please, have a look."

I stop, but refuse to turn. He must work the tourists: sell them faux-pearl rosaries, fool's gold pendants, or mass-produced garments.

Tiny feet scurry atop loose gravel. He's walking away. Then, in the distance, the jingling of metal bracelets, followed by a loud *snap*. A lid forcefully closed on a hinged wooden box.

A hand tugs my pant leg. "Miss!"

Alarmed, I tense, then face my pursuer.

Large round eyes find mine, dark brown irises with such depth they're borderline black. He's young, eight, maybe nine. The top of his taqiyah reaches my hip, then falls slightly below when his tippy-toe hold releases. His features are doll-like: perfectly portioned, petite.

His eyes study my brooch, a sterling silver sunflower, eternally bloomed, with two rows of overlapping petals. It was a gift turned good luck charm, a rabbit's foot of sorts. I'm convinced of its powers. With the tail of my scarf, I subtly shield my prized possession.

"For you." He presents his right hand, which until now hid behind his back. Balanced on his palm is a jewelry box covered with geometric designs. The sides, intricate ten-point and pentagram stars, overlap and repeat endlessly in an infinity of dizzying lines that trick perception. Iridescent opals edge the lid, two per side, except for the front, which only has one. Seven glisten in total.

With open palms, I indicate I have nothing to give.

"No, no. Take."

The peculiar design lures me. The gems transform, deepening in color until their hue morphs to an onyx black as intense as the eyes of the boy presenting the relic. Their depth is unbound, each one a hole I imagine plummeting into, a euphoric freefall without the worry of impact.

Taking my hand, he wraps each finger around the edges of the box to secure the hold. "You must accept," he whispers.

I'm zapped by a static shock, the kind I get when shuffling across carpet in socks. I try to pull away, but he won't let me.

"Why?" I ask.

The sting dulls, but there's a tugging at my chest, as if a fisherman's hook impaled my heart.

The boy releases. "*You* know why, not I." His chin tilts. "Your prayer has been heard. With this, you will find your answers. If it is peace you seek, you must open your eyes."

An amplified hymn travels through speakers. The fourth prayer is called, the Maghrib, as the sun vanishes and the sky bleeds red. The boy heeds the call, touching his forehead to the mat in reverence. So young, yet seasoned and dedicated to the duty. I'm ashamed. Unsubstantiated biases got the best of me, assuming he was a swindler out for money.

I unpin the brooch and place it beside his mat. He seemed to take interest, and it's served me well. My travels are ending. It must be passed on for its adventures to continue. Now it is his.

"Let's go!" Jeffrey yells, dangling from the bus. A row of windows shows portraits of hungry scowls, displeased with my procrastination.

I feel their stares as I walk the narrow aisle.

"I didn't realize you spoke Arabic!" Eileen, an English professor, rests cross-armed atop my reclined seat, her wrist-length sleeves sponges for perspiration. Her fuzzy gray curls, victim to subtropical heat, look like a cotton ball plucked apart.

"Huh?"

"I overheard you talking with that boy. I didn't take you as a polyglot."

"A *polygoat?*"

I clutch my purse. Without knowing the circumstances, she could assume the gift was unlawful. No money was exchanged.

"A polyglot. A person who speaks multiple languages. I've studied this area of the world for quite some time but have yet to achieve fluency in Arabic. It's a difficult language for us native English speakers."

I'm confused. The boy spoke English, didn't he? She misunderstood, which serves her right for snooping. She's a professor. She can't be so batty to have misinterpreted English for Arabic.

"Be seated, please!" Jeffrey jabs the ceiling with his umbrella, retaking the reins.

"Impressive," Eileen notes, then slips back into her seat.

The lights on the bus dim, and we welcome the silence. David, a middle-aged accountant vaguely resembling Ted Danson, dozes off first and jumpstarts a chorus of heavy breathers and snorers. A nightly lullaby of worn travelers thousands of miles from home.

Again, now with privacy, I admire the jewelry box's details, tracing its labyrinth of lines and shapes. I flip the box, seeking a clue, any clue, revealing how it could help. Scrawled on the back, just below the hinges, is calligraphy: entwined letters, cramped for space, like I once observed in the Book of Kells. A poem, only four lines, etched into the antique olivewood. I read the words once, and then twice. It's a peculiar poem, and not at all comforting.

Leaning against the headrest, I close my eyes and repeat them from memory, reflecting on their significance.

Our eyes can capture wonders, flashes of sublime.
Eternity surrounds you, irrelevant is time.
But darkness casts its shadow, pain we can't neglect,
For all that we encounter is all we must accept.

Exhaustion from travel overtakes me. At a dead-end, with no more information to gather, I allow my mind to numb and remember the voices in song.

Tonight, braided challah paired with tannic red wine will lull the faithful into a state of serenity and will continue to be shared until the first star reappears with two companions in tow. Together, they will signal the Shabbat's end. Why? Because the sighting of one star may be a fluke, perhaps a mistaken planet. A second star builds confidence, yet skepticism remains. But a third star brings certainty. Three is stable. Three is secure. It confirms what the first two already know: all good things must come to an end.

1

OLIVIA, EIGHTY-EIGHT YEARS OLD (PRESENT TIME)

"Only the fortunate are granted a past," my father once said, scratching the razor burn smearing his jaw, a Milky Way of inflamed nicks and bumps sprawling from under a tight, top-buttoned collar. "You have to live long enough to have one."

Turns out, he wouldn't be so fortunate.

I was fifteen. It was sometime in autumn. His sensitive skin freshly assaulted by a dull blade and daybreak's chill, and staunchly resistant to the handlebar-mustache style of the time. It was to be his last shave of the season. Come winter, a robust beard would maturate, transforming his clean-cut appearance to a modern Captain Ahab, fearless commander of his suburban Detroit home.

I used to believe his words, that good luck brought longevity. As years passed, against the odds, I convinced myself I'd been kept alive to stir the pot, to create a little havoc, but now, I'm not so sure.

Last Friday I turned eighty-eight. Seated before a store-bought sheet cake smothered in gritty buttercream, serenaded by the voices of my caretakers, who, for the most part, were paid to be there, all I could think was, *Why me? Why am I still here?* Lives better than mine were cut short. Culture idolizes longevity, with fad diets and snake oil remedies, but what fear of mortality neglects to notice is the *price* of longevity, is loss.

My vanity went first, humbled by buckled knees and liver spots, but this year my mind decided to follow. Yesterday the nurse arrived to change my sheets. She comes every Monday, but do you think I remembered her name? Nope. I stared blankly, the chalkboard in my brain wiped clean, simply nodding politely while she tidied. Hours later it hit me: *Rita*.

Though my short-term memory's shot, distant memories have resurfaced. Faces from my past find me, lost to a greedy Earth craving change, recycling the ashes of the old to make room for new life. Each nook and cranny, bump and groove appear for a second, two at most, as if the breath sustaining them never stopped. The details are sharp, stamped in my memory with a fresh pad of ink: steep slopes of an aquiline nose, dimples on cheeks and chins. These are the faces I've loved.

I'm aware of the absurdity. Faces cannot appear from thin air like the Cheshire Cat. A doctor would diagnose dementia or perhaps Alzheimer's, same as Dottie, my sister. *Likely hereditary,* they'd say, then group me with the 5.7 million others diagnosed this year, coordinate my care to include "family support," or worse, add a drug to my overflowing pill box. Donepezil, Rivastigmine, Galantamine, Memantine: these are fine for patients with valuable years to their life, but I've accepted defeat. I treat visions like a chronic disease. I don't seek a cure because I'm willing to ride it out, and if no one knows, no one can stop me.

But one persistent image haunts me. His was the first, starting in my sixties. Clothed in thick, stiff denim, he always arrives unannounced. Stitched upon his chest are square and rectangular pockets in a Tetris-like pattern, with light bouncing off the melted metal buckles of his overalls. Unlike the others, he comes without a face, erased from the shoulders up, but I don't need those details. His presence is felt. He is a part of me.

"Hello, Dad," I sometimes say, then, a tad sarcastically, "Lucky for *you*, I've got plenty of years to share."

I HEAR THEM WHISPERING.

"Do you think she's adjusting?"

"She's new, give her time."

"But she hasn't made an effort. She never comes to dinner."

"Can you blame her? It must be depressing, seeing them drool and stare into space. She's a decade older than the others but acts half their age."

My nurses. They talk about me. I'm not supposed to hear this, but I'd mistakenly left the door ajar in the middle of the night after walking the halls. I'm used to living alone. I miss it.

"She's a sweet old lady. Reminds me of my granny. She just seems so...down."

"Does she have family?"

"A niece, I think. You saw her birthday party. It was just us. Poor thing."

I shift my weight, easing the rocking chair back. Stretching my neck to better position my ears. Gently. Steadily. Just a little more...

A blood-curdling cry rings out, shattering placidity.

Their conversation stops.

My cat's tail is pinned against the hardwood floor. He winces with teeth exposed, unleashing a primal scream.

"Winston!"

He darts past me, dodging furniture legs and staggering in pain, leaving a lump of grey hairs stuck to the rocker's curved bottom band. An unfinished game of solitaire scatters, sending kings and queens airborne. I flail my arms to reel him in, but it does nothing more than create a cool breeze while limp, loose skin flaps wildly.

He's a millimeter away from disaster, grazing the ashtray during a dismount from the davenport to the loveseat. One more strand of hair and he would've soiled the Persian Medallion rug, the one auctioned for a number that'd make my bank account salivate. It was a gift from my niece, Linda, whose taste is exquisite. She curates her belongings, appreciating the history within the fabric. I prefer to forget history, but Linda curates me, so the least I can do is keep it clean for a couple years until she inherits it back.

Two knuckles tap my doorway's frame. I freeze. The touch is gentle, but I'm on edge, caught red-handed.

"Everything OK in here?" This voice is deep and male. He's careful not to wake the neighbors. I squint at the source. Broad shoulders span the opening's width, draped in green, monochromatic scrubs. It's the day nurse. Behind him, a slightly older woman with under-eye bags the size of fists, whose own shift has come to an end.

"All good." Discreetly, my gnarled elbow, lacking girth, makes a sad attempt to block the ashtray on the dresser. They've discovered I'm presumptuous, they don't need to know I'm a rule breaker, too. "The cat's a little spooked, that's all."

Residents are banned from smoking in rooms, something about a Michigan Smoke-Free Air Law. We're limited to a small, plastic hut twenty feet from the main entrance, which, consequently, is a foot from the sidewalk. It's clear on four sides, perfect for a passerby to judge our poor decisions, lamenting how tax dollars will pay for our pending COPD treatments.

"You sure?" he prods, his tone serious. More like a warden than a nurse. He gives a firm, single nod to the woman, who quickly takes off, relinquishing her duties.

"I, ah..."

The dimmed lamplight catches Winton's eyes, who has taken refuge under the bed. Slowly, he scoots back until undetectable, further into the cave of lost socks and slippers.

"Yeah," I manage, distracted and remorseful. "I'm sure."

He senses hesitation and lingers. I'm new to McMall Manor, having just arrived in April. My name is on everyone's lips. The staff doesn't know what to think of me yet, still unsure of the amount of care I'll require.

"Alright then." With a suspicious smile he walks off, shutting the door behind him. Heavy footsteps creak the floor, then fade, soon replaced by Doris's Pomeranian yapping next door, roused by the commotion. Two more knocks, but this time on Doris's door.

"Thanks for blowing my cover." Winston's two beady eyes return.

Double checking that the door is latched, I slide open the top drawer of my dresser. Buried under wired brassieres is my pack of smokes, Marlboro Smooths. The nicotine works its magic. Tension lifts from my joints. I enjoy watching the white paper retreat as the irradiant orange and yellow flame grows, burning through the tiny cylinder. It's the only flame I've learned to control.

Winston prudently emerges. His feather-duster tail sashays with his stride, seemingly fine, but something's not right. He hasn't recovered. "Oh, you're alright, Win. Walk it off."

He doesn't. His head lowers to his paws, spine curved, ready to pounce.

"Suit yourself."

I watch him intently, as he does me.

Smoke circles release from my circled lips, which morph and disperse, rising toward the smoke detector in a menacing dance, one that devilishly brings joy. But suddenly, a shooting pain seizes the muscles in my hand. My fingers claw, contorting swollen muscles. The final puff becomes more of a crooked C. The spasm is fierce: a bolt of lightning from my heart to my fingertips.

Abruptly, with a *pop*, Winston thrusts forward. He's headed straight for the dresser, but his heft handicaps his agility. He's a wrecking ball aimed at antique oak, crashing into the bottom molding with a blow that rattles my treasures to the edge: my father's bifocals, my mother's amber necklace, and an opal-studded jewelry box, a souvenir from a trip to Jerusalem. There they teeter, one nudge from a free fall.

I hold my breath as the jewelry box sways.

Winston twists and flails, flopping onto his gut and knocking the cigarette from my grasp. It corkscrews toward the rug in a synchronized dive with the jewelry box.

"Shit!" I scramble to intercept the fumble and catch the stick before it splatters. The smell of burnt flesh rises, and when I look down, I see a perfectly formed circle where the cigarette tip seared, dead center on the wisdom line of my palm. The burn is no bigger than a dime and hurts like hell.

The jewelry box bounces until landing upright, then bustles like a teapot, whistling with built-up steam. The lid bursts under the pressure.

A blazing light emanates from its silk-lined interior and engulfs the room.

Tears drip from my ducts, my eyes involuntarily forced shut. Finally, a reprieve as the intensity lessens. The room turns pitch black, aside from a single stream of light, unifying from the opals and connecting with my palm's fresh, agonizing burn.

"Win!" I wave my hand, blindly seeking my dresser, but instead smack my wrist against a cold brass bar. Toilet paper spills from its reel. My movements are fluid, my posture straight, my tender, swollen rheumatic joints relieved, and even more than that, healed. Gradually my vision readjusts to decipher objects and colors. I'm sitting on porcelain with underpants down to my ankles, locked in a bathroom stall. Winston is nowhere to be found.

I wear a silky black skirt, sloppily hinged with a safety pin. It's my mother's, lent for the occasion, clasped around a slight waist with child-like hips. I recognize the pleats. In fact, I recognize it all, these slender hands with their chewed nails. These nubby breasts still waiting to plump, but they should come in nicely in another year.

Today is my father's funeral. This body is *mine*. I'm fifteen years old.

I peek under the stalls for feet but find none. "Hello?" I ask meekly. No response. My own voice is clear in tone and almost unrecognizable, not yet affected by the smoke-induced nodules that will form on my vocal cords.

The mirror above the sink greets me with the face of my youth. Brown, wavy hair tangled in knots from a sleepless night and indifference, despite my mother's pleas to have some decency and show everyone we're OK.

We're not OK. I haven't left my bed since the explosion, and consequently have transformed into a sliver of myself, having lost ten pounds on a frame that couldn't bear to spare it.

My collapsed eyeballs show the brunt of it, sunken-in a good inch, like I took two knocks straight to the sockets. They're accentuated by puffed cheeks, sore and tender to the touch, hidden beneath the layer of black netting that adorns my charcoal pillbox hat.

"Ol?" The creaking door stops when gapped an inch. A small voice travels from thin lips pressed against the heavy wood. "Ol, are you still in here?" It's my younger sister, Dottie.

I lift the netting and splash my face, hoping the cool water tames the red, and then, determined to be rid of every tear, tightly pull the skin of my temples until my eyes are slits. "Yeah, Dot?"

"We're getting a crowd, Ol." It's softer yet, if possible. She's nervous to upset me. She's been nervous since Dad passed, too worked up to mourn. She's been Mom's shadow from dusk to dawn, her knobby, stocking clad knees always one step behind.

"I'm coming, just gimme a minute." A drop of crimson falls onto the sink and bleeds into the running water, thinning and dispersing until meeting its fate in the drain's abyss. The scab's split open. A warm, moist circle expands from my elbow, sticking my sleeve to the newly healing skin. I wince as each movement rips the cloth's bond.

The hallway teems with men and women here to pay respects, wearing visual proof of their despair—bombazine, parramatta, merino wool, and cashmere—all dyed to the deepest black.

I pin my back as close to the wall as possible, cursing the fact that I hadn't shrunk another dress size. Maybe then I'd completely disappear. I tug my hat's netting until it grazes my upper lip, praying it renders me invisible. They gather in tight circles while waiting to greet my mother, pitying our bad fortune.

"*Such a shame. A true shame.*"

"*His young wife and daughters left without support.*"

"What d'ya suppose she'll do? Surely she can't work."

"She'll have no choice. You can't live on kindness forever."

They speak of my widowed mother, only thirty-six, but who could pass for a woman ten years her junior. Having spent her days in the home, her tongue prefers her native Polish and only engages in American pleasantries like "Good morning" and "How d'you do?" If she's caught as the recipient of the latter, she promptly ends the conversation with a nod and forced smile. Now, she stands before the casket doing just that, not because she can't *find* the words, but because there *are* no words.

I spot Dottie among the mourners. She's the focal point of Ms. Kushner and Ms. Koski, our frail, bone-thin neighbors, who both began their eightieth year recently. Their black lace gloves hold tissues against their nostrils, the delicate fabric frayed near the fingertips, worn from funerals past. They shower Dottie with condolences while imprisoning her tiny face atop their ridged sternums.

Inching along, my right shoulder suddenly loses support. I've run out of wall.

My patent leather shoes, a size too small, cut circulation to my toes, making me clumsy. I fall backward, desperately grabbing hanging coats and scarfs.

Dazed, I'm tangled in a sea of wool, sprawled on the coatroom floor. I try kicking free, but like a Chinese finger trap, the more I kick the tighter they restrain. Loose wire hangers shred my good hosiery which, like the skirt, belongs to my mother. Defeated, I can feel tears swell.

Suddenly, two white satin gloves divide the overhanging coats that cling to the rod, then, before I can resist, clench my wrists and yank me forward. I'm thrown to my feet, exposed for all to see.

Concerned faces find me, the poor, lost girl who'll forever be in their minds when they mutter the phrase: *it could always be worse*. Their jaws dangle, fit to nest a bird. The woman with the satin gloves doesn't take notice, but instead picks up the coats, humming a subtle, colorful melody. "There." She pats away the dust. "No harm done." Then straightens the shoulder pads, lining them neatly back onto the rod, one by one.

"Goodness, dear, you're bleeding!" She rolls my sleeve until it clears past my elbow, then pulls gauze from her coat pocket. I turn away, flinching from the sting. She ties a black handkerchief around the wound. "That'll do for now. Be sure to wash it tonight, then wrap it tight. Find a nice, cold steak if you notice swelling."

"Thank you," I mutter, my gaze locked down. If I avoid eye contact with the crowd, maybe they'll move on.

But this woman refuses. Gently, a long, supple finger lifts my chin. "Olivia, is it? Darling girl. Are you well?"

I'm bothered by the idiocy of the question. What does she think? I'm at my father's funeral. Though resistant, curiosity grabs me. I look up.

Her beauty steals my breath. Vibrant blond curls spill from under her headscarf, refusing repression and bouncing with the slightest motion. She looks in her thirties, though younger than my mother. Her skin is flawless, without a detectable pore, but it's her eyes that demand attention. They're a soothing lavender, with hints of blues and gray absorbed by deep, black pupils. She smirks, and as she does, a chestnut brown mole, perfectly placed to the left of her lip's crease, dances on the high-set bone of her cheek.

Seeing that I'm cared for, conversations resume, instantly making me grateful for her attentiveness. She tucks a loose strand of hair behind my ear. "Show your pretty face, dear. You only get this one once."

An odd comment, but I manage a smile, sort of. "Thank you."

She bends down and swivels my leg to find the nylon's run. "For shame. I'm afraid that's unfixable. You'll need a new pair."

She unzips her clutch. "Here." In her hand is a sterling silver brooch in the shape of a sunflower. "Surely you wish to feel glamorous on such an occasion. This will suffice for now." Without asking, she pins the gift over my heart. "Wear it proudly," she instructs. "May it remind you each day to always stretch toward the light."

She cups my cheek in her palm. The heat generating from her body strengthens, like a finger left on a hot stove. I'm forced to turn away.

"I'm sorry, dear." Her hand quickly retreats, but before she can hide it, a bluish purple glow shines through the satin. "I'm a bit flush, I'm afraid."

She bows her head, her golden curls bidding adieu. "Don't give up, my dear. If you search for peace, one day it will find you."

Then, as if finding a secret passage, she slips into a sea of carnations and escapes through the side entrance of the funeral home.

The silver brooch is freshly polished and sparkles in the light streaming through the stained glass. I'm left unsure, but somehow, eased. The twinkling petals lure me. I tilt the flower's head to examine the intricacies, and then—

Another flash of light, equal in intensity.

I'm back in my cramped apartment, staring at wrinkled feet.

"Winston..." I graze the tips of his coat. Tiny spikes tickle my fingertips. His fogged, gray eyes are apathetic to my bewilderment. I study my charred palm. It's just as I left it. Two perfect circles, one inside of the other, the smaller one with endless depth returning my gaze.

My lungs turn concrete. I can't breathe. Tears form streams in the wrinkles of my cheeks, carrying pent-up pain.

"I'm losing my marbles," I confess, but Winston's no help. He cleans his coat while I sit in silence, waiting for an answer from a taciturn animal. This wasn't like the flashes of my earlier hallucinations. Unlike before, the images continued, building upon one another to create an entire scene from my past, like a movie projector reeling film.

The jewelry box has repositioned itself at the base of the bed, a good foot from the dresser where it fell, silently taunting, *No one will believe you*. But, do *I* believe me?

I wait for movement, the slightest twitch. Nothing. Paranoia sets in. Am I being watched?

Hanging above my headboard is a replica of da Vinci's *Salvator Mundi*. Jesus's right hand gives a benediction for divinity, his left holds a crystal orb, and his two listless, yet eerily life-like, eyes follow my every move. The painting was a gift on my confirmation. A bit mature, and unsettling, for an eight-year-old child if you ask me, but I guess it's never too early to introduce the lifelong battle with Catholic guilt. "Here kid, this man died for you, he gave his body as bread, so don't you dare miss a Sunday morning mass."

The night the painting was mounted, my mother insisted we christen it with prayer. I knelt before the oil-based Lord with a doily slapped atop my uncombed hair, hands clenched in devotion beside my mother. *"Zdrowaś Maryjo, łaski pełna..."* She swayed, speaking in her native tongue.

Now, in desperation, I find myself praying again. The phantom scent of incense and recently re-varnished pews tickles my nose, and then a new smell, almost musty, but not quite. Kind of like—

"Smoke!"

I push Winston aside. "Move it!" He sprints to the door and I wobble behind.

The smoke billows in the bedroom and the flames spread quickly. I open the door to let Winston run for help. The fire alarm's triggered. An ear-piercing siren lets everyone know the new lady in room B20 set her place ablaze.

We gather outside, our slippers damp from the morning dew. The staff accounts for us all. "Lorraine! Maxwell! Estelle!" We're an army of slouching white-haired soldiers. Beeping watches are reminders to take our morning medications.

A man lurks at the end of the line. He's older, like us, but not quite. He carries a youthful energy. Energy us residents once possessed, but were stripped of in exchange for lodging. His face is foreign to me, as is his attire. He's dressed for the heat, wearing a white linen button-up over taupe cotton pants. His shirttails flop when they catch a breeze. He's staggeringly tall. He doesn't seem to care that he's noticeable. He holds his chin high, observing the scene with a sharp sense of authority.

Slyly, I bend behind Lorraine for a better view.

"Lorraine!" I whisper, needing verification. I've lost faith in my wits. Lorraine's distracted. I lean in, closer to her ear, and find the battery door of her hearing aid is pried open. For God's sake, she's deaf. If I nudge her she'll startle and draw attention.

The man ducks and stretches to track the firemen as they extinguish the flames and start clearing the rubbish from my room. Clothes, furniture, cat food. A pair of unworn, pristine Isotoner slippers are added to the pile. I cringe. What a waste. I might as well have set a fifty-dollar bill on fire.

"Ma'am," a stern, baritone voice booms. A fireman. He holds a shoebox.

"The place is wrecked," he says. "The smoke damage is pretty bad. All of your belongings are covered in soot, except these. Anything in here you wanna keep?"

He removes the lid and shows me a half-filled jar of nickels for the casino, a glass paperweight with an entrapped carnation, and a miniature, resin Boyds Bear—a get well present from the manor after my hip replacement.

"Toss it," I order. I despise tchotchkes.

"What about this?" A second fireman with a baby face prances toward us. Freckles cover his skin like spilt coffee grounds and lead to a mop of shaggy auburn hair. His enthusiasm and lack of chin stubble are giveaways that he's the new guy.

He holds the jewelry box, untouched.

"That too."

"But ma'am, this is in perfect condition." He's confused and deflated. His dropped jaw displays horse-sized gapped teeth. I've squashed the pride behind his valiant act of property salvation which, given his age, is probably his first.

I shake my head.

He turns, his face long, and baseball throws the jewelry box into the dumpster.

Finally, I'm able to breathe.

I don't know why these lucid visions come, but that last one was the mother of them all. I have no proof. No video of what occurred. That jewelry box may have been in the wrong place at the wrong time and is now taking the blame for my declining mind, but my gut doesn't tell me that's so.

I've been a fool, swindled into believing an empty promise that night in Jerusalem. I was vulnerable, and the boy knew it. It's laughable really, to believe a jewelry box could bring peace. It's a *curse*. It must go —the box, the memories, the underlying hope—all of it. And, unless I learn to start faking competence, I can kiss my independence goodbye, too.

Remembering the new man among the residents, I turn back. He's vanished. I scan the parking lot, but there's no trace of him.

Franklin, the manor's veteran security guard, emerges. His puffed gut tests the strength of his shirt's buttons. With a twist and a tug of his belt he saves his pants from dropping. "All clear!"

White-haired friends shuffle in, a parade of senile, over-medicated zombies looking forward to a breakfast of cold eggs and gummy sausages. One by one, miffed eyes find me as they pass, and their precarious, painfully slow pace causes their glares to linger.

Winston finds me. He maneuvers figure eights around the legs of my walker. Together, we take a minute.

"Ma'am." It's the fireman again, the mature one. He stands tall, shoulders squared, surely prepared with a lecture. My head hangs low to avoid eye contact. This isn't my first fire; I'm well aware of the danger and how quickly the situation can escalate.

"Are you OK?" His voice is soft, concerned.

There's a tugging at my chest and a gaping, likely infected wound on my palm. I'm not OK, but I don't say these things. Instead, mortified, I squeeze my hand into a fist and nod, masking discomfort. "I will be. Go on."

Grabbing the porch rail, I pause on the concrete ramp. Winston does, too. With a heavy heart, we glance at the dumpster, now brimming with ashen, mangled possessions. Among the rubble is a sparkle

—scintillating aquatic blues and teals—sunlight reflecting off the curved surface opals.

"Good riddance."

Winston jumps over the threshold, and I follow, resolute in knowing I will no longer look back.

2

JUNE, TWENTY-EIGHT YEARS OLD (PRESENT TIME)

A glass bottle of Chanel No. 5 sits atop the fireplace like a first-place trophy sandwiched between the family portrait and an antique pendulum clock. The iconic design, with its clean, beveled lines, still holds the ounce of fragrance Grandma Dottie never used.

Unlike the rest of the decor, which has fallen into seasonal rotation, the perfume stays put. It became Dottie's signature scent—a spritz in the morning, and another before bed. Mom placed the bottle on the mantel immediately following the ceremony without saying a word. Neither did I. She wasn't ready to let go, and likely still isn't, but Great-Aunt Olivia's arrival has given her a new purpose. Maybe it's her nature, but Mom isn't 'Mom' without an object to nurture. And, I get it. It's her drug. Love is like any other addiction, when the fix is gone we seek another to fill the void. Where Mom and I differ is, she ignores the warning signs of the first fix's end, then blankets the grief. Not me. I like to watch a train while it's coming at me. I've been blind-sided before, and it's not going to happen again.

A hollow chime rings flat as the clock strikes 6:45. *Is it morning or night?* I've been awake for hours.

I tiptoe pass Aunt Olivia's room. One ear against the door, I listen for sounds of life. A creaking bed frame and the rustling of blankets eases concerns. Gently, I pry it open. Olivia's shadowy outline is barely visible against blackout shades, her drooping chin projecting a soft, whistling snore. She's sound asleep.

The living room's a mess. There are hundreds of me sprawled on the shagged carpet. A lifetime documented in photos. Every blemished, over-exposed image captured through a disposable camera's lens. Overstuffed albums, acquired from the cedar closet, flood the couch. Being an only child defaults me as Mom's favorite muse.

"What the hell was I thinking?" A chunky, glittered belt clings to low-rise blue jeans. I flip the page. It's no better. A too-small Abercrombie and Fitch shirt proudly flaunts my pre-teen midriff. I came home to reconnect with my roots, but this attempt at feel-good nostalgia is backfiring, making me more depressed.

Then, Olivia's smile, gleaming from a shiny four-by-six print, redeems the effort. It's a rarity. Seeing Olivia's lips curved in an upward fashion is equivalent to spotting Bigfoot. That's not to imply she's never happy; quite the opposite. She just doesn't fake it. To her, charity-chuckles for terrible jokes are disingenuous, and "*enable more bad jokes*." But this occasion was special. This smile was real, and I'll never forget it.

I hold a diploma, standing before the graduation stage. Bobby pins painfully secure an awkward, square-edged cap to my scalp: the cherry on top of a glossy red robe. The ceremony was over, but I wasn't feeling celebratory. That fall, while my friends stuffed U-Hauls with second-hand furniture, I'd be at home, in my childhood room, preparing for community college. The reason wasn't academic: it was financial. I refused to be Mom and Dad's scholastic money-pit and chose the cost-effective option. Olivia had caught wind of this. Tired of me sulking, she pulled me aside. "The best of you is yet to come," she said, two fists full of cheap red fabric. "Your circumstances don't define you. Your actions do."

Despite how I felt about myself, she was proud of me. She said what I needed to hear, and I believed her. But now, as I'm once again inhabiting the childhood room I can't escape, I find it ironic that the defining action of my life seems to be stagnancy.

A vibration tickles my hip. Tucked in my robe's pocket is my cell phone. The lit-up screen shows a text message. Of course. It's Mom.

Day shifter called off. Stuck at work until coverage comes. <3 you.

Despite our differences, my mom's a saint. A strong-willed, good-for-everything woman that I need more than air. She didn't flinch when her boomerang daughter needed a place to stay, and shortly after stepped in as Olivia's legal guardian when a fallen cigarette nearly set McMall Manor up in smoke.

I inherited her uneven collarbone and widow's peak, but little else, and certainly not her work ethic. She's in her fifties but doesn't shy away from twelve-hour nursing shifts at the University of Michigan Hospital. As for me, my track record of being "asked to resign" is laughable, but in my defense, this past year hasn't gone as expected. Holding down a job was the least of my worries.

Exhausted, I slam the album shut. The breeze tussles fine, uncombed hair over my eyes, blocking what little light the room holds. Sensing a stillness, I begin my habitual morning inquiries:

"Good morning, God. Are you listening?"

I'm twenty-eight, an adult by society's standards, and yet, I remain torn between a conservative upbringing and a desire to go spiritually rogue. Lately, that desire is on fire.

"Is today the day? Will you spill your secrets?"

Patiently, I've waited for that answer. If every textbook eventually releases a new edition, how did an archaic collection of scriptures written by fewer men than I dated in high school stand the test of time? "Heaven and Earth will pass away, but my words will never pass away," says Jesus, according to Luke, by way of the Christian Standard Bible. This was repeated ad nauseam at home, but it seems to me, if I've learned anything from the childhood game of telephone, the further a message travels from the source the more convoluted it becomes.

Still, there are moments in life that dictate our conduct, that encourage us to act or think a certain way, even when new evidence challenges our reasoning. For me, one stands out.

It was November 1, All Saints' Day. I awoke to a whisk tapping a mixing bowl. My dad was making pancakes, unusual for a school morning when time constraints meant freshly toasted Pop-Tarts, but this day was different. We were to read essays touting the accomplishments of a Catholic saint. I'd chosen St. Teresa of Avila.

"Buenos dias, Santa Teresa!" Dad beamed. "I bet her father didn't send 'er off without a balanced breakfast."

Groggily, I joined the table. "She was Spanish, *Dad.* I doubt they had pancakes."

"Well, she got her strength somehow. She was a mighty woman, masterful with a pen. Did you read her work? It's important to study her writings if she's going to be your alter ego."

The batter sizzled as it hit the oiled pan.

"*His Majesty pulls up the weeds and plants good seed,*" he quoted, dancing to the rhythm of the words.

"Yeah, I guess." I sipped my orange juice, freshly squeezed, another unusual treat. "But, Dad..."

"Yes, honey?"

"If women were such good writers, how come the Bible didn't include them?"

He checked the batter for bubbles. "I don't have an answer for that. Perhaps because it was a different time. But no one's stopping you from adding to it."

"Sister Mary Ellen says the words are perfect and they don't need edits," I sharply countered.

He thought for a moment, tapping his chin with the spatula's blade. "Well, Sister Mary Ellen has some strong beliefs, and that's OK, but perhaps if you're not ready to make changes, you should challenge your understanding." He flipped the pancake and, confirming both sides were golden brown, carefully balanced the warm disc atop a towering stack.

Unsure of my dad's expectations, the next morning I took his advice and began my conversations with God, asking Him for clarification. Now, eighteen years later, like a modern-day Tevye I uphold that tradition. I find the conversations grounding, or so I tell myself, but as frustration builds and no answers come, I question my motivation.

"Hey, little buddy." Aunt Olivia's fat, geriatric cat navigates the minefield of photos to find me. His rough tongue grates my knee. An innate act, like a baby to the tit. It's nearing seven o'clock, his scheduled breakfast.

He takes the lead, waddling to the kitchen. He's lived here a week and has already identified where food is stored.

Mom's allotted space in the pantry for cat food, and it strikes me that *everything* has its place. Living here, I was accustomed to the organization. Boxes and boxes of cereal displayed label-side up in alphabetical order. Grains in bulk—amaranth, barley, buckwheat, bulger—poured into clear containers with handwritten expiration dates. Spices arranged on a wire rack, again, neatly stacked. Anywhere you look, it's symmetrical, systematic perfection.

But that's what Mom does: control. If it's within her power, she'll design a method that pleases her. And if she has no say, she'll find a way to add input. That's why Grandma Dottie's scent fills the home, and Dad's possessions are untouched. His freshly pressed suits hang in the closet, waiting for a man who'll never return. In Mom's mind, she's living life as she sees fit. Then there's me: a complete mess. She has no control. And it kills her.

"Here ya go." Dry pellets spill into his bowl, but the bag slips from my half-alert, careless grip. Cat food skids across the floor like marbles. On hands and knees, I shovel piles of chow toward the trash. Winston's unbothered, engrossed in his meal.

I reach for a dustpan, but the swift motion brings a dizzying sensation. It worsens when I stand. Nausea builds. I pray it fades. This feeling is not new. At first, I tried to ignore these spells, telling myself I needed to drink water, or get more sleep, but when they came more often, I couldn't play dumb. It's called orthostatic hypotension, the result of a sudden drop in blood pressure, usually from dehydration or lack of nutrients, that in my case is both. Just research "bulimia."

I don't keep much down nowadays.

My throat is raw, my tonsils swollen. The creases of my mouth are scabbed over, dry to the point of brittle. A glimpse at my reflection in the curve of a spoon shows the layers of bubblegum-pink lip balm have turned me into a circus clown with a distorted, disproportionate forehead.

My arm tingles, numbed. My vision goes dark, then returns, and then dark again, until finally the syncope resolves. Weak fingertips clasp the counter for support, but in doing so, accidently bump a metal canister set near the edge.

Crash.

Winston, in the wrong place at the wrong time, suffers a blow to his hind leg, exploding into the air like a furry firecracker. He may be plus size but his reflexes are fine.

He whimpers at my feet. Guilt drops me to my knees.

"I'm sorry, buddy. I didn't mean to, I..."

Defeated, my shoulders collapse, banging the cupboard door and rattling the stainless-steel pots inside.

"Dammit, June. *Again?* You fuckin' did it again."

I'm appalled. It's not how I wanted to spend the night—bent over a toilet, crippled by anxiety—and yet, that's exactly what I did.

Winston nuzzles my thigh. My exposed, cramped legs flop on the cold linoleum tiles. "Thanks, Win," I say. "I needed that."

The lush hairs of his feather-duster tail massage my cheek as he slithers away, and as he does, the silhouette of his thick frame saunters against a faint, blue glow. Light is spilling through Olivia's wedged bedroom door.

"Huh?" As I inch closer the light intensifies.

But I'd peeked into the room seconds prior. There was no night-light. The shades were closed. The light narrows until it becomes a beam, and then...*disappears.*

The doorbell rings, followed by a single, forceful knock.

I tense. My arms stipple with goosebumps.

Another knock.

"Jee-zus!" I exclaim, now annoyed. "It's early, give me a break."

Winston scats under the wingback chair. He glares at me, demanding the identity of the morning disruptor. "Your guess is as good as mine," I retort. "Maybe Mom forgot her keys?"

Atop the counter, the coffee pot gurgles charred liquid. Final bursts of steam fill the container with a dark, slosh-like brew. "*Of course.*" I'd forgotten to switch it off, but it'll have to do. I grab a mug to fill, but it's scalding, too hot to sip, so I depend on the smell to liven my senses.

Reaching for the door's cast-iron knob, I let out an obligatory, "Helloooo."

No answer. After a brief pause comes a long, heavy exhale.

Impatient, I drag the door inward and peer through the thin opening. As the lines of a face come into focus, the freshly filled mug spirals to the floor. Hot coffee splashes upward, splattering to the height of our knees, soaking my robe and his dark-wash jeans.

"Dammit, June! What was that for?" He leaps back, chanting vulgarity.

"Oh, wow, I'm so sorry." My knee-jerk reaction is to apologize, but it's short-lived once the shock wears off. "For fuck's sake, why are you here?"

"Good morning to you, too, June-bug."

There he stands. The man who proposed marriage over a meal of oysters and tiramisu, said "I do" under cathedral stained-glass, then left me alone with a million questions and extensive self-doubt. My estranged, but not yet officially ex, husband.

God, are you still listening?

"What do you want, Anthony?"

3

ANTHONY, TWENTY-EIGHT YEARS OLD (PRESENT TIME)

She looks like hell. A dab of moisturizer and swipe of mascara would do wonders, but her face is bare. Sores anchor the creases of her lips. A spider web of blood vessels spreads across the whites of her eyes like she just woke up from an all-night alcoholic binge. I should know.

If I squint, she could pass for having bed-head, which can be attractive, like when we were seventeen. She'd sneak into my room in the middle of the night, then tiptoe down the hallway with a bouncing mop of untamed hair the next morning, being careful not to wake Aunt Elaine. I'd stay under the covers, admiring the swaying dimple above her Victoria's Secret thong, always red, and always lacy.

"What?" She's clutching her robe, guarded.

My pits are drenched. The cotton of my shirt clings to my skin and is swallowed by my stomach rolls, but thankfully, or obnoxiously, my uncontrolled repetitive blinking is distracting her, a nervous tic I developed in middle school. The symptoms preceded my last panic attack, and I'm hoping history doesn't repeat itself. *Keep it together, Anth...*

"What are you waiting for?" She's staring.

I'm waiting for her to slam the door in my face. When I last heard her voice, it was enraged, filling my cell phone inbox with slurred scorn, drunkenly recalling a detailed timeline of my infidelity with footnotes of how it crushed her. *Screw you, asshole*, I recall. *Rot in hell, and take your girlfriend with you.* I'm risking my life being here.

I spill what I hope are the magic words. "McMall Manor called and said Olivia left this in her old room."

I present the jewelry box hidden behind my back, the same way I used to surprise her with flowers or the fortune cookie from Chinese take-out. She loved those crispy soothsayers and their nonsensical predictions, and I loved her smile.

This thing resembles an artifact from an archeological dig. Delicate, geometric stars embellish the wooden case, with a border of pricey-looking gems that must be fake.

"Beautiful," she remarks, then hands it back. "But how'd it get to you? You're not her power of attorney. My mom is."

"James called me, said this box looked like something special."

"Who?"

"C'mon, you know James..."

Her eyebrow arches. She's going to make me say it.

"The best man at our wedding."

"Ohh yeah, of course. James. We don't speak anymore." She studies the cuticles on her nails. "Anthony, I don't have the time or energy for this." She begins to close the door, but loses steam before the latch locks.

"Listen." I push back. It doesn't take much effort.

With an exhale, she tosses her head back. Through the gap I see her lips moving. I rest my ear against the wood grain. "*God, give me strength.*" She's...praying?

"James is the activities coordinator where Olivia was staying," I add. "He says the other day a woman came asking for her, but for privacy reasons he couldn't disclose her new address. I guess things got weird. They later caught the lady in the dumpster diving through

Olivia's damaged junk. When security went to investigate, she was holding this. James said it looked expensive."

The door's gap widens. One curious eye re-examines the offering.

"June, our friends don't know about our split. We've kept it private so far, and I didn't want to air our dirty laundry now. He called me to pick it up and I agreed."

"You mean you wanted to save face? Do me a favor, drop the box and get out of here." She bites her lip to suppress anger or frustration, likely both. The doorknob jingles, loose on the spindle, once again preparing to shut me out.

"Wait!" It's a plea.

"You couldn't have done a ding dong ditch?"

"No, I couldn't."

"Are you doing heroin?"

"God, June. Stop it, of course not." I'm self-consciously aware the dark circles encasing my cratered eyes are comparable to a junkie's, but I'll defend my sobriety; it's currently my only redeeming quality.

"June..." I reach into my pocket for the newspaper clipping.

The true reason I'm here is because June gets me. She's been the only constant in my life. The jewelry box landing in my hands was the perfect opening. I hold the clipping chest high, pinching the corners like a grenade seconds from detonating. It's an obituary for Robert Binkowksi, a man who lived in a drunken stupor and gave me nothing, aside from his damaged DNA.

My throat constricts. I've yet to say the words out loud. "My dad died."

4
JUNE, TWENTY-EIGHT YEARS OLD (PRESENT TIME)

"Oh, shit."

It's him. I've only ever seen him a couple of times, and he never looked that dapper, but it's definitely Anthony's dad in the newspaper obituary.

The black-and-white photo was taken in his teens. He wears a two-button tux with a flower boutonniere pinned on the lapel, dressed for a school dance. His hair is slicked back with something shiny. He flashes a crooked smile with a full set of teeth, soon to be extinct. In his older years, Robert's gummy mouth clamped down so hard his underbite ate his cigar.

"How do you feel?"

Anthony nudges my hip with the jewelry box, a cue to take it. "I haven't decided."

I take the box with both hands, which frees his to refold the newspaper. He transforms it into a fan, brushing his palm before returning it to the safety of his pocket.

I don't know how I feel either. Robert wasn't a doting father, or a father at all, but as long as he was alive he had potential, and Anthony held onto that potential. It's clear he's distraught. He'll never have the chance to hear "I love you" from his dad or even an "atta boy."

"You don't have to know how you feel," I say. "You don't have to know right now...or ever."

"He was a jackass," he blurts, anger rising.

Who could blame him? Anthony's adolescence was devoid of the carefree happiness a child deserves, a stark contrast to mine. My parents were helicopters. His couldn't maintain sobriety long enough to maneuver a bike.

His mom's most stable relationship was with narcotics, ironically making his dad the more responsible of the two, yet still non-existent. His dad's sister, Aunt Elaine, attempted to salvage whatever chance at a decent life Anthony had by becoming his primary caretaker. But her sweet demeanor was almost *too* agreeable, overcompensating out of pity. A child requires a certain degree of discipline that she could not provide. Love was all she had.

Now, despite what he says, Anthony can't let it go—the abandonment, the resentment, the insecurities—but it's a battle he can't win. He holds a grudge with a dead man.

"Yeah, he was."

"Still sucks." He drags the toe of his dirty, white Converse sneaker across the cement, drawing an imaginary line between us, then turns toward the front porch steps.

"Come inside, Antonius."

It's the name on his birth certificate, a name only a confidant from his past would know, appropriate given the circumstances. Our parallel lives since youth are the driving force for this olive branch, an invite into my sanctuary, my rehab—rehab from *him*.

It's difficult to close a window to the past: to shut out someone who understands better than anyone what has formed you and what has scarred you. Given that he's standing at my front door delivering this news, I have to believe the feeling is mutual.

"I'll pour you a cup of coffee."

His arched, bushy eyebrows question the offer.

"I know I suck at making coffee. I haven't gotten into fancy French press, or pour-overs, or whatever smug method you use, but I swear this pot is drinkable."

He cracks a smile. "I'll be the judge."

I widen the door's opening.

"His entire life," Anthony continues, staying put, "we only stood in the same room for an hour...tops. I'd scramble to find a topic of interest, just to get a full sentence out of him. I didn't have a clue about half the shit he was into. I researched Pink Floyd 'cause I saw him wear a shirt from their tour once, but it didn't mean a thing to him. 'That's nice, son,' he'd said. Shouldn't that have been *his* job? Shouldn't he have been asking *me* the questions?"

Anthony is still my husband technically (until the papers go through), but he was once just the boy next door and my neighborhood accomplice. We moved to Ann Arbor around the same time and grew up three houses down from one another on a block overcrowded with blue-hairs. I found him placing pennies on the railroad tracks, then scolded him for the stupidity of the act. At ten years old he could have given two shits about my thoughts on what he did for fun, but the confrontation led to us talking, and by the end of summer, we'd become inseparable, a mini Bonnie and Clyde. Decapitated tulips and skid-marked yards from bike tires were the start of our mischief making. Looking back, I would have locked us in our rooms, but my parents always felt sympathy for Anthony. I later understood why.

"Is there a service?" I ask, even though I can guess the answer.

"Are you kidding? Who would go? The body is still at the morgue. I'll be lucky to get there before it's disposed of."

"Have you claimed it?"

The situation could not be farther from my experience. When my dad died we held a proper Catholic service, and the line to offer condolences extended around the building. I'm gutted with him gone, but find comfort in knowing his soul helped create my own, and that it lives on. It must. I can't allow the alternative to be true, that he's simply *gone*.

"Not yet. I'm going back and forth. It's been less than twenty-four hours and I'm not sure I want that responsibility. He lived off the grid and probably wanted to die in obscurity too. Still, I have this image of his lifeless body on a cold metal table with his toe tagged 'unknown.' He's a real S.O.B. but his blood runs through me."

My first time meeting Robert was also Anthony's. We were thirteen, playing *Mario Kart* and eating peanut butter sandwiches, crusting Nintendo controllers with sticky fingers. Winter was on its way out and spring was in bloom. Anthony's Aunt Elaine was gardening the first round of vegetation.

She came into the kitchen unexpectedly, midway through weeding, smelling of fresh-cut grass and body odor. "Anthony, come with me, please," she said. Her tone was out of character, a flat affect without a trace of her usual hesitation.

I remember Anthony glancing at me, unsure if he should go or shrug her off. I was equally uncertain, but after a few seconds, I managed to mouth, "*Go*."

She brushed residual dirt onto her garden apron and took his hand, leading him into the backyard. Her grip tightened, giving Anthony a squeeze, indicating, "It'll be OK." I ran to the nearest window.

Standing next to a beat-up 1966 bronze Chevrolet Caprice was a lumbering man in his mid-thirties. Full head of chestnut-brown hair with a stalwart stare, as if he was Leonardo DiCaprio's less attractive brother. A piece of metal caught the sun's light and gleamed brightly around his neck, which I later learned was a gold cross he wore. The bottom of his oversized carpenter jeans flared over soiled Reebok pumps. He was fixated on jangling his keys, never stopping to observe Anthony walking toward him.

"All right, Big Shot. Here he is. Your boy." The biting sarcasm in Aunt Elaine's announcement seemed to catch Robert off guard. He stopped for a moment to pat the top of Anthony's head, then scratched the back of his own. The awkwardness was unbearable, even from the kitchen window.

Robert looked him up and down. "You turned out all right," he said, finally breaking the silence. But less than a minute later, he was back in his car with the keys in the ignition. Anthony was bewildered, to say the least, looking at Aunt Elaine for answers.

"Who was that?" I heard him ask. At thirteen, a child has the smarts to decipher when a situation's aloof, and that qualified. "That would be your father." She pulled his head against her chest and kissed the top, as if to replace the apathetic pat with a warmer memory.

Years later, in an art history class, our instructor presented a painting by Gustav Klimt entitled, *Mother and Child.* It was déjà vu. A reminder of Aunt Elaine's blanket of curls engulfing Anthony's scrawny, pre-teen frame, and for the first time, exposing her maternal instincts.

Today, that same innocent boy stands at my doorstep.

"Is the coffee still hot?"

5

OLIVIA, EIGHTY-EIGHT YEARS OLD (PRESENT TIME)

"June, is that you?" My weak, raspy voice falls short. Frustratingly short. She can't hear me. The burn on my palm screams for a cold compress and stirred me from sleep. The sight is grotesque, as new skin scabs over the ulcerated, fleshy wound.

The air carries a burnt coffee stench, fit for a drain and not for a throat. June's woken up every day before the crack of dawn since I've arrived. We both crashed back into Linda's life thanks to unforeseen circumstances, but June's two-month headstart has, inconveniently, given her a sense of responsibility for me. It's a shame, a sweet soul dealt a shitty hand, but if she's expecting pearls of wisdom as payment, I have none to give.

Winston creeps in, licking his chops.

"Someone had breakfast already, eh Winnie?" With three sources for a good meal and a few extra table scraps, Winston's making out well in his new arrangement. Nearly burning down McMall Manor was the best thing to happen to him.

Footsteps come from the kitchen, clunky and labored. They don't belong to June.

"June?" I try again, this time as pitchy as a banshee's shrill. The footsteps multiply, and then stop. I kick the volume up a notch on my hearing aid. "Shh..." Winston's licking is distracting. "Not now, Winnie." Muffled voices come from the kitchen, one being June's and the other a man's. Through split curtains I find a dilapidated van parked in the driveway, a 1999 Honda Odyssey whose rusted silver frame makes Linda's pristinely kept home look like trailer trash.

"It couldn't be..."

Sliding into my satin slippers, I grab my walker and head to the kitchen. The tennis ball grippers permit a sneak attack, quietly skidding across linoleum tile. "That little shit," I mutter.

Winnie, clued in on the mission, scurries between the walker's legs, hastening the pace of his wobble to take the lead. I find them gathered around the kitchen island, June pouring steaming brew into my mug, but it's not intended for me.

"Well, look what the cat dragged in," I announce, inspecting every inch of Anthony. His comfort is not my concern.

June nearly drops the pot, spilling a trail of hot coffee. "Jesus, not again..."

"And I don't mean Winston," I clarify. "He has *standards* with his kills."

I barely recognize him. The separation took its toll. His shrunken shirt swallows his armpits and cases his fleshy biceps like two sausages. He tugs the hem where it creeps above his belly button, revealing blotted, brown stains on the lower half.

He's a far cry from the spunky twelve-year-old with a hideous rattail that flapped when he rode his bike. I was visiting the Thursday Anthony moved in with Aunt Elaine on 14th Street, three houses and one empty lot down. I've watched him and June grow together, and eventually fall in love, or at least June did. Anthony doesn't know what love is. For a moment, he had potential. I was hoping he'd break the cycle. It's a classic battle of nature versus nurture, and in Anthony's case, we discovered that sometimes what's born in us can't be beaten out with a stick.

The coffee spill spreads. June dashes for a paper towel and the movement exposes her boney scapula in the neckline of her robe. She's emaciated. It wouldn't be absurd to think Anthony's body sucked the fat out of hers.

"You look like the Pillsbury Doughboy."

"Aunt Ol, please. I invited him in." June comes to his rescue, but I'm not convinced. She may have opened the door, but Anthony's a smooth talking manipulator. He initiated this and got what he wanted, like always.

Anthony raises his hand. "It's OK, June, really. She's right. My beer gut ironically arrived after I gave it up." He pats his belly like a shopping mall Santa Claus, lovingly caressing the sugar cookies within. "How's the hip, Olivia?"

"Hurts like hell, but I'm still breathing."

That reminds me to sit. Between an arthritic hip and a throbbing hand, I'm a mess. The Neosporin has done nothing to heal the wound on my palm. Dr. Keller, an imperious man with a ridiculous bow tie, warned the healing process would take a while. He accused me of being a non-compliant diabetic, with my blood sugars consistently reading in the two hundreds, but what does he know?

"Will you be staying for breakfast?" I ask. His answer determines if *I* will.

"No, no, I'm not staying." He braces himself with the table, beginning to rise. "I stopped by to give—"

"Anthony learned some bad news this week," June interrupts.

"Ah, yeah," he stammers, clearly not the ending he expected. "I did." He eyes June, hesitantly lowering back onto the stool.

"Join the club." I remember that a week ago I was living independently, well, *technically* it was assisted living, but it was peaceful. Visitors had to buzz the intercom before entering, and I had the option to fake a nap.

"Aunt Ol, his father passed away."

Anthony is silent. He bows his head and nods, acknowledging the news as truth. I sense the reaction's authentic.

"How'd you find out?" I ask. "I didn't think you stayed in touch."

"I don't...Well, I didn't. I read the obituary in the paper. Classic Dad, never knowing what he's up to until after the fact, including dying." He places the newspaper clipping on the granite counter. I take a glance.

I never met Anthony's father, but his reputation preceded him. After June's father passed, Linda and I shared Sunday dinners. We had just sliced into the lasagna when Robert graced the Local 4 News. There was an armed burglary at the 7-Eleven on East Jefferson, near Chene. The bandit made out with $3,000 and a case of Budweiser heavies.

Behind the reporter, a man wearing a ripped Detroit Lions Starter jacket clung to drawstring pants with the string yanked out, soiled boxer briefs the only thing hiding his ass from metro Detroit. He leaned against the storefront glass, one leg perched on an overturned paint bucket, his elbow balanced on top of his thigh, while his free hand brought a cigarette to his lips and intermittently scratched his ball sack. He gave a sly wave to the camera, unashamed of his circumstance, as if the world had the problem, not him. "That's Robert," Linda had bemoaned. "What a piece of work."

"Do you know what got him?" I scoot in to view the evidence.

"Congestive heart failure according to the write-up, but I have a feeling that was the straw that broke the camel's back. Name a bad habit and he had it."

I reach for the paper, but am stopped by a shock radiating from my forearm to my elbow, just like before. I clench my jaw to absorb the pain. It quickly subsides, but leaves my bandaged hand crippled with clawed muscles. I tuck it behind my back, but not before June notices. *Not here,* I silently beg, *not now.*

"Aunt Ol, are you—"

"Lengthy write-up," I interject.

I know she's concerned, but June will tell Linda, and Linda will heighten the surveillance. I'm one incident away from having a baby monitor installed

Loudly, I read, "Robert Binkowski, 55, of Detroit, passed away on

July 10." I can't decipher past the bold-lettered headline. The rest is in small, blurry print, and my bifocals are still on my nightstand.

But then, *poof*. The room goes dark.

My vision blurs and flickers, fighting to readjust. Limply, I skid down my chair.

June's focus intensifies. Her face shrinks, with slanted brows scrunched toward pursed lips, the wrinkle between her eyes thick as a marker's streak.

"Who submitted this?" I ask. My aim is to divert Anthony. June's attention is locked.

Thankfully Anthony's preoccupied with the obituary. "My guess is a church group, or some non-profit. The poem's probably taken from a stockpile of grief books kept at the mortuary for unclaimed bodies. I'm surprised they didn't use the Serenity Prayer. He was sentenced to so many Alcoholic Anonymous meetings he could recite it in his sleep."

I nod, only half-listening.

I tap my right cheek, assessing for a stroke, *hoping* for a stroke. There's no drooping, aside from the typical sagging skin that accompanies aging. My speech is steady, not slurred, from what I can tell. It's a disappointment. A stroke is an involuntary condition to be treated—or do me in, which may not be a bad thing—but if a flashback is pending, then I must face the facts. With the jewelry box gone, it's my mind that belongs in the dumpster.

"June, I think I need to lay down."

She nods, anticipating the request. She returns the coffee pot to the warmer, then approaches with a soft, empathetic smile—silent encouragement telling me it's OK.

"Wait!" I stick my arm out, stopping her.

Above Anthony, swirls of blues and greens project onto the oak cabinets, as if the kitchen's submerged underwater.

"What is *that* doing here?" The polished opals set in olivewood lure me, the source of the dazzling light.

The jewelry box is on the counter, near the sink. I forgo the walker, causing my ankles to quiver under feeble joints, but I stagger forward, fueled by fear.

"I brought it," Anthony discloses, standing tall with his hand on his chest.

My knee buckles and I stumble. He catches me at the waist.

"Get away from me!" I order, and swat his arm. The burn on my palm is unbearable, as if dunked in a cauldron of scalding water. "You really got a lot of nerve, you know that? You're a thief!"

There's no other explanation. The jewelry box was pitched. Its final resting place was a pile of dusty, gray rubble. Surely, he's using the box as leverage. He's not considerate, he's conniving, and now I am certain that darkness follows this evil amulet. Why else would Anthony be here, but to rehash old wounds and inflict pain on June? *That little shit*. The jewelry box doesn't belong here, and neither does Anthony.

"What? No. I, I didn't...." Anthony begins, but June pushes him aside, putting one arm around my waist and the other under my elbow for support, a nurse's hold, like she's witnessed her mother do many times.

Alarmed, he steps back, his temper rising. "You're welcome! Believe it or not, the manor called *me* to pick it up. If it means that much to you, maybe you shoulda taken better care of it. I try to do something nice and *this* is the thanks I get?" He smacks the wall with an open palm. "Coming here was a mistake."

He collects his keys and heads toward the door, but before he reaches the hall's threshold, a flash of light engulfs the room.

Time stops.

The morning sun hides and the room goes dim. The gemstones, that moments ago reflected light, now emit their own, radiating swirls of neon teals and blues. Their brightness augments and dulls in rhythm with the pulsations of my—once again—throbbing hand.

The three of us, jaws dangling, admire the show, hypnotized by the colors.

June inches closer and examines the glowing relic while the rest of us watch. She picks it up, awestruck. "Does it always do that?"

She shakes the box like a Christmas present, and as she does, a light clunk is heard, an object knocked against the interior walls.

"June?" Anthony mutters, apprehensive. Slowly, he creeps back one step into the foyer. He looks to me, blindsided by her fortitude, but I'm as lost as he is.

"June, why don't we talk about this?" I propose.

She ignores me, enthralled with the gems. She inspects the box, each side, and then flips it over. "There are words on the bottom." She recites the poem aloud:

"Our eyes can capture wonders, flashes of sublime.

Eternity surrounds you, irrelevant is time.

But darkness casts its shadow; the pain we can't neglect,

For all that we encounter, is all we must accept."

I join in on line two. At first it's involuntary, but by the fourth line I willingly continue, charmed by nostalgia. The poem's words come easily. Our voices duet, her clear tone with my weathered vocals.

Behind us, Anthony is farther away, now fully out of the kitchen.

June unhooks the latch. "There's something inside." She pulls out a crumpled wad of paper, then flattens its creases with the meat of her palm. When it levels, her eyes double in size.

"Aunt Ol, how'd you get this?"

I lean in, confused. I've never seen the paper before.

Winston, eager to investigate, bolts past my feet, his rotund tummy knocking my ankles out from under me. It's a slow-motion dive as the room holds its breath for the inevitable crash. I reach for the junk drawer's handle, but my bandage catches and unravels on the brass corner. June clutches the jewelry box like a wide receiver and uses her free hand to catch my fall, vaguely evoking the Heisman trophy pose.

She makes contact with my bare flesh and unhealed wound, palm to palm, and when she does, a bolt of lightning transfers from my heart to hers, shocking our bodies. And then, *we're gone.*

6

JUNE, SIXTEEN YEARS OLD (TWELVE YEARS AGO)

"'The only thing necessary for the triumph of evil is for good men to do nothing.'" Ms. Tomkins slams the chalk against the board's metal shelf. A mushroom cloud of white dust settles on her navy, A-line skirt. "Who said this?" she asks.

The room is quiet. There are no volunteers. Katie slouches at her desk, but her intentions of going unnoticed are sabotaged.

"Don't be shy, Katie," Sean teases, the only senior assigned to the junior-level curriculum class. He needs one more religion credit to graduate and considers the opportunity to torment his baby sister a bonus. He knew, as we all knew, Ms. Tomkins's seating chart is always alphabetical. She's a creature of habit and consistent to a fault, the only teacher who wears a student's uniform, and because she takes extra care to press and polish, she makes us look like slobs.

"Any takers?" She paces the front of the room, her slicked-back hair in a bun that bounces to the click of her heels. The smell of incense lingers from the morning's prayer.

Morality and Justice is third hour, the last class before lunch. The classroom is one of only four that overlooks the courtyard, giving a view of a stone-carved Mary, our Lady of Grace, with palms upturned and arms spread wide. Her head clothed and bowed in reverence to her Holy Father, whose role oddly doubles as the father of *her* child. There's a submissive, almost vulnerable quality to her chiseled eyes.

"Edmund Burke!" Anthony yells. He's the last seat in the row of Bs, farthest from the chalkboard.

Surprised, I turn in my chair "Say *what*?"

"Right!" Ms. Tomkins's gobsmacked expression mirrors mine. We're both pleasantly caught off guard. "And what do you think it means?"

He doesn't expect a follow up question. "Uhhh...well..." He shuffles to straighten his posture, tapping his pen against the faux-wood desk. "Just as it says. If we don't stand up for what we believe in, evil will take over." Pleased with his answer, he nods, and in doing so convinces her, *and* himself. "Yeah. That's it."

Ms. Tomkins crosses her arms. Her slender fingers loop the circumference of her petite biceps—lean muscle that has never lifted more than the weight of a textbook.

"And what do *you* believe in?" she pries.

All thirty pairs of eyes lock on Anthony. The boy who never speaks is now in the hot seat. Ms. Tomkins is relentless and taking full advantage of his out-of-character participation. He thinks quickly.

"Isn't that what I am here for? For *you* to tell *me*?" He arches forward, challenging her inquisition.

The lunch bell rings. "Thank *Gawd*." Anthony doesn't wait to be scolded for blasphemy. He's the first one out of the room. The rest of us hold our breath. But Ms. Tomkins doesn't give us the satisfaction of a reaction. Instead, she shakes her head and erases the chalkboard, creating a clean slate for the next group of students.

"You get the fries and I'll get the Skittles." Katie zips her backpack, then jogs to the lunch line. "I'll save a table." She disappears into the pushing stampede of navy blue and khaki. We rotate who buys what; since the fries are $2.50 and the Skittles a buck and a quarter, the cost evens out by the end of the year.

I walk out to an empty hall. All classes have been dismissed, and in the distance are the echoes of overlapping conversation:

"Did you bring your practice jersey?"

"That was due today?"

"Can you believe it?"

"That's what I heard..."

But as the clatter settles, other sounds emerge—a high-pitched quiver, followed by sniffling, and then hyperventilated breathing. It's a girl. Her muffled whimpering mimics a caged bird.

An overstuffed bookbag sticks out from a row of lockers—forest green, with the JanSport logo. The girl senses my presence and mutes to protect her solitude. I wait. She stays silent. With another step, more of the bag's details become visible: a collection of last season's admission tags to Mount Brighton, and a keychain with a hand-stitched ichthys—the Jesus fish—saying, "Forbidden fruit creates many jams."

"Michelle?"

Michelle Kowalski is the middle child of seven, and the third to pass through the halls of St. Vincent's. The family is a staple at Sunday mass. Matthew, their eldest, is annually assigned the role of Joseph in the *Christmas Nativity;* they host Father Tom for wine on weekends; and they donate loads—and I mean *loads*—of cash to the diocese. Their quarterly endowment paid for the new gym floors and cafeteria chairs, and we're reminded of their generosity every morning when passing a cast bronze plaque that caps the front entrance. *Vernon Kowalski*, scrolled on the top. *I can do all things through Christ who strengthens me*, trims the bottom, and in the middle, an etched portrait with a dark oxide finish illustrating Michelle's grandfather's face. Just a few more checks and the school will be renamed.

Despite jealousy giving me every reason not to, I've always liked Michelle. She's a classic overlooked middle child, the quiet type that lives below the radar, modestly keeping her skirt knee-length and buttoning her Oxford to conceal cleavage. She's precisely what was intended with the uniform's chaste design, unlike Katie's version, which doesn't leave much to the imagination. Michelle and I went from acquaintances to friends after being partnered in anatomy to compose a clay version of the human muscular system, which we agreed resembled an emaciated Keith Richards.

I inch closer. "Michelle, it's June."

She hastily wipes the moisture off her cheeks. "Hey," she responds, despondently. Grabbing a chunk of her auburn hair, she splits it into three and proceeds to braid, further blocking her face, which already hides in a shadow. Her knees compress her chest.

"Are you...OK?"

"I'm fine," she snaps. Aside from contorted fingers, she's perfectly still. Even her breathing has leveled.

Normally, I respect personal space, but Michelle's detached behavior is such a stark contrast to her usual, outgoing ways that I have to know what's up. Plus, if the situation were reversed, she'd wait. So, I wait.

She forgoes the braid and collapses into the fold of her arms.

I inch closer. "Can you believe Anthony? I've barely heard him say two words in that class, and then he comes up with *that*? I didn't know he had it in him."

It's small talk, but it's something.

"People have plenty of qualities that may come as a shock." Her head rises from the nest of her arms. Her mascara is smeared across her temples, dragged by tears. She's gnawed her lower lip, the skin dried and flaked, a dismal sight compared to her trademark lip gloss shine. "What's evil anyway? Seems self-righteous to claim to know. Who made Burke God?"

She hurls her backpack against the wall to use as a cushion, crushing the brown bag lunch inside, then moans after hearing the damage. Once again, her eyes swell with tears.

"Michelle, I don't know what's going on, and I don't need to know, but would you like me to take you to the counselor, or—"

She adamantly tosses her head side to side.

"Stop!" she wails. Then, more softly, controlled, "Just stop." She sucks her lips until the pink disappears. Her flushed face restrains pending hysteria as she quietly counts breaths like sheep. She makes it to five.

"If I tell you something, promise to never repeat it?"

I nod, because I have no choice. If I say no, I must go, leaving her stranded. But, if I say yes, I consent to the request.

"I had a miscarriage." Her affect is flat, lax, and near lifeless, like her body. She might as well have complained that her mom packed a bologna sandwich.

"Woah, I, uh...." I didn't see that coming. "I'm so sorry, I guess? Did you want a baby? I didn't realize you were pregnant, I—"

"*Don't.*" Once again, her face takes refuge in her palms; she pushes words through squished cheeks. "I'm glad it happened."

"Who, uh...I mean...who's the..."

"The father?" She breaks into a tear-laden laugh. "I knew you'd ask."

"I didn't think you were dating anyone."

"I'm not. Like I said—" Her back slides, inching lower until her head's height equals her knees. "People have qualities that may come as a shock. Even teachers." Her tone turns sarcastic. "Let's just say the kid would've been great at math."

"Mr. Stuart?" I immediately cover my mouth. Her eyes go wide, her face pale. She's appalled by the outburst. She scans the halls to ensure no one's snuck up on us.

"What are you trying to do?" She pulls her legs closer, tightening her human ball.

"Sorry, it slipped, but holy shit, Mr. Stuart? He's, what, forty? Doesn't he have a family?"

Mr. Stuart's attractive. He looks younger than he is and has style, with glasses so nerdy they make him cool, accentuating his chiseled, dimpled jaw. He's consistently top three in Katie's flippant, slumber-party entertainment, *Teachers I'd Bang*. But that was hypothetical, or so I thought.

"Forty-four, and two kids; a wife, too, I guess, but he said they're ending it."

"A divorce?"

She shrugs. "It doesn't matter anyway. Since there's nothing to worry about, he doesn't need to know."

His kids, a son and a daughter, attend the elementary school whose graduates feed into our high school. His oldest, Isaiah, became an altar boy last Sunday. Mr. Stuart beamed with pride watching him carry the thurible, swaying it so hard he choked on incense. His wife seemed equally pleased, her perfect roller curls brushing his cardigan as she laid her head on his shoulder. From the outside, their marriage appeared solid. No signs of trouble. I get the feeling Michelle's been deceived by pretty words.

If the scandal went public it would rock St. Vincent's. Besides teaching algebra, Mr. Stuart is the football team's defensive coordinator, reaching idol status after the team was state champions two years running.

"Well, shit," I mutter. Speechless.

The window beside us faces the west side of the courtyard, the same one viewed from our classroom. From this angle, Mary's profile is in view and we can see her delicate nose and dainty chin.

"Look at her." Michelle touches the glass. Steam from the heat of her fingertips fogs the surface. "Confident in the path that was chosen for her. God gave her a son and she said, 'Sure, bring it on.' Where's my angel telling me I have 'found favor with God?' I would have felt a hell of a lot better about it."

"Have you seen a doctor?" I lean against the sill.

"Sarah took me." For the first time since I found her, Michelle makes eye contact. "I said, I'm *fine*."

Sarah is Michelle's older sister. She's a freshman at Hope College, a Christian-faith institution on the western side of the state. She was also the head of our high school's Right to Life club and raised the funds for students to travel to the march in Washington D.C. On more than one occasion I've seen her camped outside Planned Parenthood with a sign reading, *Does your doctor kill babies?*

I awkwardly pick the chipped pink polish from my thumbnail, uncertain if I'm helping or making the situation worse. "Well, if you need anything, don't hesitate..." but when I look up, I stop. Michelle's checked out, gazing off at the holy, maternal sculpted stone.

She repeats the phrase from class. "'The only thing necessary for the triumph of evil is for good men to do nothing.'" "That's what we're bred to do around here, right?"

I shrug, relinquishing words.

She continues, "We're told to be the 'good' that does something. To be the moral army that graduates from these four walls to stand up to an evil outside world that performs abortions and supports a marriage that can't procreate. We're meant to be the carrier of the light, to fight for the meek, to be the voice for those who don't have one." She takes a breath and collects herself. "But what about *my* voice? What if *I'm* the meek?"

I'm in deep. I was expecting she was dumped, but now my brain is hustling to keep up. "The miscarriage wasn't your fault. It wasn't meant to be."

"Enough!" she pleads. Her penny loafers kick the nearest locker. The noise of smashed steel vibrates down the empty hall. I'm stunned, exhausted from vacillating emotions.

Her expression melts. "You sound like Sarah. 'Your baby's in heaven. God knew you weren't ready.' She hasn't a clue about the details. She's like a fucking script from a grief counselor. But what if I'm not grieving? What terrifies me most is what I would have done if the miscarriage hadn't happened. What side of the fight against evil does that put me on? What if I was the one my sister handed a brochure to, telling me there are other options while she sits pretty, heading to college on a full ride without a human growing in her uterus?"

"Michelle, you're a good person."

"Am I?" she challenges. "I thought I was, but now I don't know. For eight weeks I considered doing what I never thought I would."

With a hop, she secures her bookbag straps onto her shoulders, then knocks on the glass with her knuckle, motioning to the courtyard and the statue surrounded by chrysanthemums.

"And what about Mary?" She twists the button on her cardigan latched above her belly button. "Her body was capable of growing a child, lucky her. So, she had to change her plans, but what if she wanted to start her own revolution?"

The sound of a falling pen breaks our focus.

"Great." She rubs under her eyes, wiping the smudged mascara clean. "Now the whole school will know." She darts toward the cafeteria and doesn't look back. The rosary strung onto her backpack zipper bangs her plaid skirt as she runs.

Waiting until she passes, Anthony steps out from the cove of the classroom doorway.

"So *that*'s why." He watches Michelle round the corner, then walks to meet me.

"How long have you been there?" I demand.

"Long enough to hear Michelle's little secret."

"This is none of your business."

He hands me a crinkled loose-leaf notebook paper with bubbly teacher's penmanship. Written in the top margin is the author and the chalkboard quote, and below it a string of bullet-pointed questions with intentions to spark conversation among students.

"You cheated?" I feel foolish for giving him credit. Of course he didn't know the answer.

"It was face-up on Ms. Tomkins's desk. She made it easy. No one else was saying anything." He shrugs off my accusation.

"But you hate speaking in class. What made you care?"

He bends to pick up his pen, the mishap that gave away his hiding spot.

"Michelle was crying into her sweater sleeve. She kept it down, but then the room went silent while Ms. Tomkins waited for an answer. She held her breath to stay quiet, but I'd give her a minute before she popped a lung. So, I said something."

The bell rings. Metal chairs hit table legs and the soles of sneakers squeak. Conversations grow louder as students flood the halls. Lunch has ended, and my stomach is growling.

Anthony takes off. Halfway to the corridor, he stops and reaches into his cargo pockets. "Here!" A granola bar smacks the tile and skids to my feet. "Take it. I have an extra." He smiles and then disappears, leaving me alone in the hallway.

I wonder when word will travel about Michelle, because despite our best efforts, it will. Anthony bought her time by taking the heat in class, maybe a day or two to collect her thoughts, but soon the world will tell her what she should believe, or how she should feel.

I crumple the paper. If I hadn't stumbled upon Michelle, I would have called Anthony a little shit for cheating, condemned his character for falsely appearing knowledgeable when others in the class actually studied. I would have said something I'd regret, something biting, based off a short-sighted assumption—a snippet of the bigger picture.

What if there are fluke instances in life when a little evil contributes to the greater good, like when a stolen answer sheet saves a terrified girl from the sharp lashings that come from teenage tongues whispering behind her back?

"June!" It's Katie, with an opened bag of Skittles in hand. "I saved you the reds."

I slide the paper wad into the waistband of my skirt.

"What happened? I was going to come get you but Emily got talking about her date with Eli and I couldn't leave."

She continues to give details of the date—their shared plate of pasta primavera at the Olive Garden, Eli's attempt to feel Emily up before dropping her off at home—but I'm not in the mood to listen.

"June?" Katie snaps her fingers. "You all right?"

I nod and force a smile.

The second bell rings, the last call.

Bodies rush past, faster and faster, nudging my shoulders from both directions. I'm pulled into the river of students, dragged with the masses, until the colors blend into to a chromatic, blinding white. Suddenly, a bolt of lightning strikes my chest, transporting me from my youth.

7
ANTHONY, TWENTY-EIGHT YEARS OLD (PRESENT TIME)

"Uhhhh...June?" I call.

No response.

Winston stands at the feet of their paralyzed bodies, head cocked, waiting for an explanation. I inch into the hallway from the foyer and stretch my neck for a better view, for signs of life. The flattened, wrinkled paper lies on the counter, exactly where June left it. Olivia's got a death grip on the jewelry box.

"June?" I repeat. She doesn't flinch.

I take short, steady steps. Now in the kitchen, I circle their bodies. June's is stiff, her bulging neck muscles flexed to the point of snapping. They age her, and show the extent of her neglect for nutrition. Her elbow is double the size of her bicep; the round, boney joint stretches her thin skin like pizza dough. I push her shoulder, but quickly pull away. "Damn!" Heat from her body scorches the flesh on my fingertip, turning it bright pink. I watch as the ridges smooth, then line-by-line reemerge to form the maze that is my print.

My breathing shallows. My nerves tangle. I'm queasy and need to shit. My instincts urge: *get out*. I retract my steps but am stopped by the cold, hard counter. My hip rams its edge. That'll leave a bruise. A gust from the force of the blow lifts the crumpled paper. It glides down like a feather, supported by the resistance of air, and lands within my view. The black ink has a metallic shine, emitting a faint glow.

"What the..."

Suddenly, June's body pops.

Her chest puffs as she gasps for air. Her back bends like it was smacked with a baseball bat. She's hurled off her feet and onto her tailbone. "Oooo," she moans. The linoleum takes a beating. I cringe too, like watching a sports blooper where an outfielder hits the fence.

Olivia follows, a much softer return, directly atop June's lap, sitting snugly between her thighs and hips. Their eyes are glassed over. The jewelry box is jarred free, then lands on Olivia's gut, showcased like a crown on a pillow.

Frightened, Winston sprints and attempts to leap into my arms, but his weight impedes his vertical jump. He knocks the back of my knees instead, but I manage to snatch the paper before my ass pounds the tile. All three of us are sprawled on the floor in agony.

"Aunt Ol..." June speaks, barely, straining for air with Olivia's elbow pressed against her windpipe. Olivia massages the nape of her neck, slowly coming to her senses. She's awkwardly bent, her back curved from osteoporosis. She takes the cue from June's grimace and scoots off her chest. The vibrant blues and teals of the jewelry box's gemstones have darkened into an inconspicuous pool of black, no different from rocks found along a shore.

June is trembling. She tries to tighten her robe but doesn't have the coordination to tie the rope. She forfeits and clutches the fabric. Managing to kneel, she grabs the counter to pull herself up. Frazzled, her wild eyes scan its surface. "Where'd it go?"

I hold the crinkled loose-leaf paper high as ransom. I'm not sure what kind of witchcraft or prank is going on but I want answers. "What the hell just happened?" I demand.

"Give me that!" June leaps for the paper but I move it out of reach.

"OK, real funny." I assume she'll drop this nonsense, but her breathing doesn't slow. Her ribcage struggles to exhale the entering air before the next batch comes. "First you make up that creepy poem, and now you plant this note from high school? I knew you were pissed, but *really*, June? Get over it. We were teenagers."

"Anthony, I *didn't* keep it! I haven't seen that since we were sixteen. It was in the jewelry box! Listen to me, something really weird just happened." She's pressing on her chest. "Feel. My heart is pounding." She squats beside me, then grabs my hand and places it near her breast. Inside, her heart beats her ribs like a drumhead, like she's been stabbed with a shot of adrenaline.

"I was there," she says. "I was back at St. Vincent's. You were there. Michelle was there. Remember her? Ms. Tomkins was there." She squeezes my cheeks. Her speech is frantic. "It was real—as real as you feel now. After the flash of light I felt a shock, but it didn't hurt; it was like a dulled bee sting. Then, when the light dimmed, I was sixteen again, and I..."

"Come off it, June!" I push her hands away. Her eyes are pleading, glistening orbs begging to be believed.

"Listen to her, Anthony," Olivia orders, breaking her silence. She's at the table, flustered, trying to rewrap the bandage but her hands are too shaky. She chucks it on the ground in defeat, a new toy for Winston, who quickly pounces. "I was there. I saw the whole thing, through June's eyes."

She pats her pockets and finds her box of Marlboros, but a violent tremor jostles the last cigarette before it reaches her lips. It rolls under the refrigerator. She chucks the empty container across the room and substitutes Winston for comfort, nervously mangling his fur.

"You shouldn't have brought that here," she says, her tremor slowing, her attention focused on the jewelry box now at her feet.

"Why not?"

"Because without it, none of this would be happening." A single drop of sweat glides down Olivia's chin. June inches closer. "Aunt Ol, what do you know? What are you talking—"

"*Listen to the words*," she barks, her patience short.

Shocked, June's jaw lengthens, eyes bugged. She *expects* Olivia to be feisty with me, but to her, a sharp tongue has only been used as a weapon of defense, never in attack.

The corners of Olivia's eyes are weighted, regretful. "'But darkness casts its shadow; the pain we can't neglect,'" she recites, softly, now overcompensating. "The jewelry box *brings pain.* Its sorcery started with flashbacks, visions and scents from the past. They've plagued me for decades, but now, we are *reliving* the moments in their entirety, experiencing the pain of the wound on the first cut. Get rid of it. *Now.* We have no control over what will come."

"What else have you seen?" I ask, picking up where June left off. Enticed by Olivia's uncharacteristic outburst, I decide to play the game. If this is a joke, the plan is either crumbling or the performances are worthy of a standing ovation. I look to June, her eyes swollen with tears, like a child who gets their first glimpse at an unfavorable side of authority, one they've never seen.

Olivia's tight lipped, keeping her focus on the jewelry box, but one look at June and she concedes. "It was last week," she begins, clearing her throat. "Right before *the incident.*" She speaks of the fire at the manor, still too proud to admit her involvement. "One moment I was in my La-Z-Boy, then the next I was at my father's funeral."

June sniffles and places her hand atop her great-aunt's. Their eyes connect, Olivia's relaying a non-verbal apology, June's relaying acceptance.

I'm familiar with Olivia's story. Her father died in an explosion when she was a teenager. June says Olivia witnessed the whole, bloody thing, and swears it's the reason Olivia never married or started a family. Olivia didn't want to love anything she had the risk of losing.

On our wedding day, June and I put up with the usual, dumb questions about having kids, the first being from Brett Spalding, the youth minister at St. Thomas the Apostle, a Catholic church where June volunteered. "'First comes love, then comes marriage,'" he jested with a wink and an elbow jab, humoring himself. Olivia overheard. "Why bring a child into a world so cruel?" she snapped, clearing the smile off his haughty, oafish face. I never liked her more.

June says the incident with her father wrecked Olivia. She would sporadically disappear, taking off for months on end, and with no one to report to, the details of her travels were obscure. Word is, the explosion nearly killed Olivia as well, and she had a near-death experience of the transcendental kind. The family always skirted around the story, afraid to reignite difficult memories.

To be honest, I never bought it. It was a while ago, 1940-something. Modern science has a better understanding of the physiological response to trauma. Blood flow slows or is blocked, resulting in vivid illusions. A brain's activity goes haywire. The same sensation occurs when sleep deprived. The claim is proof of Olivia's intellectual shortcomings. She's always been, and apparently still is, crazy.

Olivia's lost her credibility. Plus, it's well known she hates to be viewed as incompetent; it's why she fights aging. But whether she likes it or not, she's eighty-eight years old and is here because she set fire to her assisted living complex. She can blame ghosts, or time travel, or whatever extenuating delusion she wants. The truth is, *she's old*. Her brain is rotting, and if June doesn't wise up, she'll be next in the line of danger.

"It was just a bad trip," I insist. "Your medicines had some kind of interaction."

"Then what about me?" June counters. "And the light from the jewelry box? How do you explain that?"

I shrug. "A trick switch? A hidden flashlight? I don't know," I say, then add: "Maybe she rubbed off on you. Is crazy contagious, or hereditary?"

"Watch it!" Olivia's pointed finger is millimeters from my nose. She hurls her body weight, preparing to stand. Her waist bends at a forty-five-degree angle before she keels over, curling into a ball. She moans and compresses the injured hand between her thighs. Winston runs to her aid but skids to a halt, and from a safe distance, adds trebled meows to her agonizing wails. Slowly, he backpedals, fearful of his owner.

"Aunt Ol..." June is next to try. She makes it one step past Winston when a lightning bolt of electricity shoots from Olivia's fingertips, frying the fine hairs that line her scalp.

The bolt travels to my watch, zapping the rim and popping the crown like a cork. "Dammit!" The scorched metal burns my wrist. I fling it off. The case smacks and shatters upon contact with the linoleum tile. Winston releases a blood-curdling howl when a chunk strikes his hind leg.

Stunned, Olivia makes a fist to obstruct the current.

"June!" She lifts her palm shoulder height. Her crippled knuckles expand and contract. The boil is inflamed, as if a rubber band is wrapped around her wrist. "What is it doing?!"

June leans forward. Her face flushes. "Anthony..." She quivers.

I sprint to her side and squeeze between them for a closer look. June peers over my shoulder, reclaiming her view. Olivia struggles to hold still as we examine the burn.

There are two rings, one encased in the other, almost resembling...

"Is it just me...or does it look like, like a..." Uncertain, I tilt my head to try another angle.

Before I finish, the odd shape takes on a distinguishable form. The two circles morph into an iris and a pupil, and around them, a fainter, third oval takes shape. It stretches toward the edge of her palm, below the pinky, and extends to the flap of skin where the thumb bends—the sclera. The object fully comes into being, and then...*blink*.

"Holy shit!" My head flings back and smashes June's nose.

She frantically cups her mouth. Blood dribbles between her fingers. "Jesus, Anthony!" She pinches the bridge to obstruct the broken vessel.

Olivia flicks her wrist wildly. "Get it off! Get it off!"

Unsure whom to help first, I run to grab a wet cloth. June shoves the hemmed tip into her nose and uses the other end to wipe the building tears. Finally, able to see again, she glimpses Olivia's palm. "Good God ..."

The cigarette burn has healed, and in its place an...*eye*.

Vibrant, galactic pinwheels of blues and teals fill the iris, mimicking the colors seen on the jewelry box. Tiny sparks of electricity shoot from Olivia's fingertips, a captivating waterfall of light. She stops, awed by the display, and gently, warily, wiggles her wrist.

"Move the cloth." She motions to June's battered nose.

June's terrified, but follows the order. She lowers the soaked cloth. The bleeding resumes, drizzling down and painting her upper lip. Before June can object, Olivia forcefully sticks her pinky finger into her nostril.

June winces as an electric shock cauterizes the wound. Her hair stands on end. She rubs her thumb under her nostril and it comes back clean. "It worked."

Olivia collapses into a chair and marvels at her new, bedazzling growth, until suddenly, the eye snaps shut.

There's a loud knock.

In unison, all three of us swivel toward the sound. June's the first to move. She walks toward the foyer, wiping at the blood around her mouth, then manages to let out a stifled, "Hello?"

"Would this be June?" From the other side, a voice bellows with a faint, yet detectable, Creole accent. "We need to talk."

8
JUNE, TWENTY-EIGHT YEARS OLD (PRESENT TIME)

Olivia scrambles for her walker, thrusting her body forward to clasp the aluminum leg. Her boobs are two odd lumps the shape of butternut squash. They nearly reach her waist, a burden for balance. Still, with grit, she's at the door before I can assist.

"Who's there!?" she demands, her expression sour. She pushes me aside. Her nightgown's splattered with drying blood, and visible through the garment's thin cloth is the glowing iris, poorly obscured. The eyelashes flutter when it blinks, in quick, repetitive movements that make my skin crawl. She squints through the peephole, smashing the cartilage of her nose until her pupil practically brushes its metal rim. "I can't see shit."

"Aunt Ol!" I grab her wrist as she reaches for the knob. Tiny red squiggles, electrical burns, extend from her palm to her elbow. Her nightgown is singed where her palm touched. More concerning is the steam-like smoke exuding from her fingertips.

"We need to get you to a hospital..."

"I'm not going anywhere." She yanks her wrist free.

"It could be poisoning you!"

"I'm eighty-eight years old. If this is the end, I'm fine with that.

Doctors don't know shit. Think they've ever seen a third eye sprout on an old woman? I'll be a spectacle, and you can't convince me otherwise."

"Listen to your aunty!" our visitor calls, eavesdropping. "You don't need a doctor. You need *me*. Lenny. You can't do this by yourself." The voice is fluid, almost melodic, with vowels that climb the bars of each measure. "Make me help you," he urges. "You have the trinket, yah?"

With that, Olivia flings the door open, fearless, while I try to swallow the lump clogging my throat. One look at our visitor's face and her arms go limp and dangle like a broken marionette's. "It's *you*."

Towering over six feet tall, the man is no wider than a telephone pole. A stark-white linen shirt hangs from his angular shoulders like it never left the rack. His long, thin arms form two gigantic triangles, bending at the elbow with hands resting on his hips. If they started to flap, it's entirely possible he could take flight.

His skin is smooth, aside from the delta of wrinkles that bookend his eyes, evidence of a life under the sun. A nest of grey dreadlocks frames his forehead, lushly falling from a thick hairline.

"Good morning!" he blares affably. His breath is fragrant, with the earthy musk of tobacco, but also sweet, like whipped meringue. His smile extends beyond his narrow, peach-fuzzed jaw, which squeezes together two solid rows of rounded, pearly teeth.

With nostrils flared, Olivia stands before him. "Who *are* you?"

"So, you *did* notice me?" He nods, thumb on his chin, a corner of his lip stretched toward the sky. "You caused a scene, yah? The whole place scattered." He speaks of McMall Manor and the fallen cigarette. A cackle spills from his gut into the air; it's delightful, like bursting bubbles of pure joy.

"Never mind that." Olivia scowls, her pursedsmoker's lips taking their familiar shape. "I know what happened. I asked about *you*."

Cordially, he bows. "My name is Lenny. Lenny Ambrose. Maurice's son. Alban's grandson." His right hand finds his heart. "Cleveland is home, but my roots be in Jamaica." In doing so, his lightweight sleeve slides. A scar wraps his forearm and continues to and through the crease of his thumb, as though a pencil eraser marred his skin. The tips of his fingers are calloused, the ridged tissue thick and bubbled.

"Never been." She's unimpressed.

"Then you're missing out. Going anytime is good, but from spring to winter the almond trees peak. The salt from the ocean leaks into their roots. They're the best in the world," he reminisces.

"Cleveland is a three-hour drive from Ann Arbor. Why are you here?" I ask.

Behind him, a Ford Taurus is parked on the curb. It's a modest four-door, rusted along the brim like a burnt cookie's bottom. Beads are strung over the rearview mirror—red, yellow, and green—with a dangling Lion of Judah ornament. Fierce yet regal, its mouth exhales a permanent roar, yet, atop its mane sits a three-point crown, the middle a cross, as an insignia of superior status. Stickers slather the uneven bumper, proclaiming *Power to the Peaceful* and *Out of Many, One People.* In the passenger seat, a seatbelt secures a briefcase, and on the dashboard there's a stack of notebook papers with red pen vehemently scribbled over pencil markings.

Distracted, he hovers over our heads, snaking his neck with fluid muscles that rise then drop his shoulders like a seiche of water. His finger stabs the air, finding the object of his desire. "Because of *that*."

He turns sideways, manipulating his size, and shimmies through the gap between our shoulders. He heads for the kitchen.

He spins the jewelry box atop his palm like a toy top, and proceeds to juggle it, ducking and sliding while the box dances mid-air, a high-risk game of hacky-sack.

"Hello, ole friend," he says. "Still confiscating people's souls, I see."

Outside, a thunderous rumble sounds, but the sky is clear.

The jewelry box rockets from his grip, scrapes the ceiling, then falls like a diver, landing with an ear-piercing smack. Only Lenny smiles.

"I better be quick. Lightning follows thunder!" Another cackle leaves his gut.

He motions for the table, but before sitting, pours a cup of lukewarm coffee. One sip and the mug's pushed aside. "Rass!" His face contorts. "It's bitter! Is this coffee or mud?"

Anthony sits across from him, where he's been, discreetly, since Lenny arrived. A cloth speckled with dried blood, *my* blood, cloaks his neck like a boxer's. "What did you mean by that?"

Lenny looks up.

"When you said 'confiscating souls?'"

Anthony's timid in his questioning, leery of the goliath before him. At 5'9" he appears misplaced, bumped from the kids' table and forced to sit with an actual adult.

"You must be Anthony," Lenny says confidently.

Startled, Anthony crosses his arms, guarded. "You know who I am?"

"No."

"Then how do you..."

"I know *what* you are, not *who*. Soon, you will know, too."

"Come again?"

The now signature smile spreads.

Lenny leans back. His butt scoots to the seat's edge, his legs unfolding beneath the table until his feet surpass its length. "I came to help, and that's what I'm going to do. I don't have to show you, *that* will." He nods to the jewelry box. As he speaks, his eyes glisten for a fleeting moment with indigos and fuchsias.

"I don't usually do this, just show up like this, but I'm doing a favor for a friend. She helped my grandfather."

Lenny shifts to allow his arm access to his pocket, which seems endless: a pit of clinking coins and keys. Soon he's elbow deep. "Ah ha!" But before he can do a reveal, like the flick of a switch, a beam of light ejects from Olivia's palm, zapping the earring clear off his lobe. Smoke dissipates from his crown like a blown-out match.

"Looks like I'll have to wait." He laughs, then in unsaid abidance, removes the earring's pair. The two miniature sterling-silver sunflowers are an unusual choice of jewelry for a man his age, which I estimate to be mid-seventies.

The beam of light returns, this time aimed at the jewelry box. Still across the room, Olivia turns her face, fighting to accept what's coming and clearly frustrated by her lack of control. The light fractures and connects to the row of opals lining the rim. Waves of effervescent teals and blues fill the room, buoyant tongues of color that slather the wall, and then vanish.

At the table, Lenny smirks. "Open it." He nudges the box toward Anthony.

"Hold it, Anthony!" Olivia barks. "Don't be foolish. Remember what I said: *nothing good will come*."

It's a useless attempt, for before the last word leaves Olivia's lips the lid pops open. Inside, levitating above the satin lining, is a paper wedding invitation: *We Invite You to Celebrate the Love of June Edith and Antonius Joseph.* The calligraphy branches out to form two locked hearts, the same emblem that graces my parents' invitation. Anthony looks to me. Fear floods his eyes. "Told you so," I mouth.

Warily, he lifts the wooden box to inspect for an opening, some way a paper could slip inside. But the corners are tightly sealed.

The eye on Olivia's palm's indisputably stares at Anthony.

"Enjoy the ride!" Lenny cackles, higher in pitch, almost delirious. "This isn't my journey. I'll be waiting." He gives a salute.

Anthony leaves the table, jewelry box balancing on open palms, as far from his chest as his arms allow. I meet him halfway, and together, side-by-side, we walk to Olivia. Her palm's eye is wide awake: *waiting*.

Behind us Lenny recites the poem; he knows it by heart, and then...*poof*. Three souls travel through time.

9
ANTHONY, TWENTY-FOUR YEARS OLD (FOUR YEARS AGO)

"You ready, man?" James playfully smirks, nudging my elbow. "She'll be beautiful. The prettiest you've ever seen her. Mine was."

James was the first to marry. He wed Sarah in a rustic country barn, kicking off a domino effect of weddings. For a woman in her mid-twenties, a diamond ring on a finger is like blood in the water, others will swarm and thirst for more.

I smile and nod. I want to rip off this bowtie. The wool collar of the coat rubs my neck raw. It cost two hundred dollars to rent this tuxedo and they couldn't find one made of cotton.

The conductor waves his baton for the string quartet to play. Katie, June's maid of honor, leads the procession. She's got to be fucking kidding with that walk. If she'd pull the stick out of her ass she'd get somewhere. She taps her heels together before putting the next foot forward. "For Christ's sake..."

James hears me and clears his throat. "Don't be nervous," he advises. "It'll be fine."

If he only knew. It's not nerves surfacing, it's disgust. This fulsome display is for June. All her family is here, spotlighting the fact that I have none. Even James, my best man, is more of a reliable, convenient acquaintance. June insisted on a wedding party, and wanted the number to appear balanced when standing at the altar. So, here he is.

Father Tom calmly resides before the congregation, hands resting atop his protruding belly with his chin raised like he's sniffing for treats. He's a balding, middle-aged man wearing a collar that squeezes his neck like a stress toy.

Katie throws a thumbs-up as she steps into position. "She's gorgeous," she mouths with a wink. The quartet flips their sheet music and in unison draws their bows to begin *Canon in D Major*. The guests rise in the pews and face the vestibule to catch the first glimpse.

June steps into the opening of the narthex, her arm wrapped around Linda's elbow. The veil blurs her face but her figure is svelte. The dress cinches her waist and plumps her breasts, exposing tanning-bed-darkened cleavage that contrasts the stark white fabric. James, still smiling, leans into my ear. "Told ya."

"Who gives this woman to be married?" Father Tom's voice is seasoned, fine-tuned by weekly projections of the liturgy of the Eucharist.

"We do." Linda beams, speaking for two but standing alone.

June's dad, Jack, died four years ago from a ruptured brain aneurysm at age fifty-five. He left a collection of Bob Seger vinyl, a frayed Vietnam veteran cap, a Semper Fi pin, and the honor of walking his baby girl down the aisle.

Linda steps in and lifts her daughter's veil. The Semper Fi pin secures her corsage. June dabs away a tear. Her blond hair, slicked into a tight bun, tortuously yanks her forehead smooth. The arched bridge of her nose, her father's nose, is minimized by caked on powder. Put together, it's overwhelming. She's a painted caricature of herself.

She gives Katie her bouquet and stretches her hands toward me. Father Tom begins, "A reading from 1 Corinthians, verse 13..."

Aunt Elaine occupies the first pew with fumes and pride exuding from freshly permed curls. Her acrylic, red nails leave indents on Uncle

Eddy's bicep, her baby brother and the last of the Binkowski siblings. My father, the oldest, is the only one not in attendance.

"Anthony, do you take this woman to be your lawfully wedded wife? To have and to hold—"

"I do!" I yell, startled at the recognition of my name. Chuckling spreads. Lucky for me, my momentary stupor was mistaken for excitement.

Father repeats the vows. "I do," June replies, softly.

Aunt Elaine sighs, pleased with the fruits of her labor. She's raised me since I was five, and maybe now I'll have a chance at a normal nuclear family.

"You may kiss the bride," Father Tom announces, his stubby fingers pressing the lectionary to his chest.

June meets me over halfway, her strawberry-glossed lips leave a tacky film on mine.

James slaps my shoulder. "Congrats, man."

The organ recessional music is our cue. Aunt Elaine applauds and blows a kiss. Uncle Eddy pretends to tip his nonexistent hat, and the row of relatives that follow flash wide smiles, relieved that the boy born to a black sheep has made it through this ritual of adulthood.

"Let's make some pearls out of this oyster," June whispers with a sly smile, the phrase I told her when I slid a diamond ring onto her finger, which now accompanies a rose-gold band. When I said it, through mascara streaked tears she asked what I meant. "When you're born into a world as ugly as mine, holding out for the pearl is the only thing that keeps you hanging on," I told her.

Some days, most days, I'm not sure what I'm waiting for.

There's a collective, affectionate sigh as we exit the sanctuary. I loosen my collar and unhook the top button, sucking in air with hefty gulps. But the pressure on my chest grows stronger.

"Hard part's done. After you, my man." James hands me the flask hidden within the inner lining of his suit coat. After a three-second swig I go back for round two. "Damn, son, let the buzz hit you first."

Katie rubs the lipstick off June's teeth and adjusts her train, readying her for the receiving line. She waves for me to join.

"One second." I point to the restroom.

She nods. "Hurry up!"

Sweat drips from my crotch and soaks into silk socks as specks of light dance along my peripheral vision. I slip behind a magazine rack of Sunday programs and lean against the cool wood. Ice travels through my veins, constricting my lungs and challenging my breathing. I beat my ribcage to relax the muscles.

I'm having a panic attack.

With two simple words, "I do," I solidified the path for my life. I am verbally bound to be a husband and partner. My decisions are no longer mine—they're *ours*.

I dry heave twice before the whiskey retraces its route through my esophagus, soiling the auburn carpet. When I look up my vision is tunneled, zoomed in on the light shining from the cathedral's entrance.

I squint to focus. The heat from the afternoon sun hints at a mirage, or some kind of illusion. I mold the wedding program into a bag and regain bodily control by sucking in exhaled carbon dioxide.

The silhouette of a man becomes visible. The frame of his body is familiar and the shadows make prominent his bowed legs. He's dressed in a plaid polyester suit, wearing a forward-tilted fedora that masks his eyes. His hands tuck into his pockets, high-water pants barely brushing the top of his penny loafers, and sporting a plush beard with curly-q hairs that hang from his chin. The style is so absurd it'd be chic on a younger man.

He pulls his hand from his pocket with a firm grip on a handkerchief, which he uses to sponge perspiration collecting beneath his cap. He leans against the door's frame for stability, next to an oil-painted sycamore-fig tree, a Biblical depiction of Luke 19:1–10. He looks lost.

Clinking heels grow louder, then muffle when they reach the carpet. "Anthony, what's going on? You're letting June thank the guests by herself?" Aunt Elaine finds me hugging my knees. "Anthony!"

Alarmed, she grabs a bottle of water from her purse and forces it between my lips, but it dribbles down my chin.

My eyes stay focused on the mysterious figure. "Snap out of it," she pleads. Confused, she follows my gaze and spots the object of my attention. Her face pales. "Robert..."

The man flicks the ashes from his cigar and takes a step past the entry threshold. Aunt Elaine cradles my head in her bosom and makes direct eye contact with the wedding crasher. Out of the harsh sunlight, the shadows from the brim of his hat disappear, revealing two beady eyes. He turns his gaze to me, shrugs his shoulders to adjust his coat, and then stops.

Slowly, he retreats.

Aunt Elaine rocks me back and forth, as if I were once again a boy, and unconcerned that my size dwarfs her petite frame. I pull away and start to rise. The man turns his back to us as he walks toward the sidewalk, not bothering to take another look at what he left behind.

"Let him go." She brushes dust off her sequined dress. "Your dad came, and that's more than I expected. It may not be what we want, but it's what he can give."

With the man gone, there's nothing to block the midday sun from entering the hall. I close my eyes, relaxed by the gentle rocking, numbed by the light's warmth. I let it take me, and just like that, my soul escapes.

10

JUNE, TWENTY-EIGHT YEARS OLD (PRESENT TIME)

Anthony's forearm pins my neck to the floor. Olivia lands belly down on his chest, adding to the piled-on weight. Her palm's eye is wide open, observing its wreckage.

I manage to dislodge my tangled limbs and skid to freedom.

Olivia moves next, grunting and scooting on her elbows to dismount Anthony, careful not to disturb the eye. She leans against the cupboard and lets her arms go limp as a ragdoll's. She begins swallowing spit, eventually losing to her reflexes. Vomit heaves into her cheeks, but she quickly gulps it down and expels a wet belch, which seems to bring relief. Nausea is a nasty side effect of the trip. She's on number three.

Anthony moves last. Quietly, he makes his way to the table to take a seat. His movements are mechanical, his expression insentient. He digs his forehead into his wrists and self-soothes with a rocking motion, tottering at the waist.

Reason tells me not to, it was beyond my control, but I feel guilt. Our wedding day, what I very clichély bragged to be the happiest of my life, and what I assumed to be his, was the last moment he saw his father alive. I had no idea, and at the time, neither did he.

"Are you OK?" I ask.

He looks up, then quickly reburies his face.

"Anth?" I try again.

"June. Don't!" He drags his nose across his collar, leaving a skid mark of snot.

I'm taken aback, but I shouldn't be. It's classic Anthony. He wants attention on his terms and deflects when he feels vulnerable. I get it, he's upset, but his irritability doesn't do him any favors, and subconsciously triggers the combative component of my personality that awoke with the words "I do."

I want to expose his frailty, psychoanalyze his feelings and demand that he communicate them, but that didn't work when we were married and it won't now. He bottles emotions while my heart is boldly displayed. It's a conflict of catharsis that had me convinced I was an inadequate partner, and left him frustrated with my incessant need to empathize with afflictions he considered to be transient and irrelevant. "*Let's talk about it*," I'd beg. "*Tell me what's wrong*," I'd insist, but he'd rather gnaw his arm off.

I want to, every part of me wants to, but instead, I drop it. We're not married anymore. He can figure it out.

Winston hisses and claws at Olivia, cautious of her new, fluttering eye. The sleepy lid droops and prepares for hibernation, and then, it finally...*shuts*.

Lenny sits legs crossed atop the counter, posed while presiding. Preoccupied, I'd forgotten he was here.

"Anthony," he calls, the top button of his shirt undone so the sun touches his chest, turning spiraled hairs into a web of glowworms. A shadow slices his face in two.

Anthony's swaying stops. His hands drop, revealing aggravated, bloodshot eyes.

"Yeah?" he answers flatly.

Mere moments ago, a magical jewelry box was still theoretical to him, observed but not experienced. Before he became the next victim.

"Here, my boy." A mangled plastic bag rainbows over the island and drops onto Anthony's lap. "Ginger sweeties. Sailor man's medicine." He fetches another, equally crinkled bag from his pocket and rips it open. This one he keeps, smacking his tongue as the gummy starch sticks to his teeth's enamel.

Anthony nods—a thank you—but he sets the candy aside. Four red streaks mar his collarbone, scratched raw from jagged fingernails, one of his many anxious tendencies. He used to maul his body like it was covered with fleas, determined to rid his skin of every demonized, imaginary one of them. His shoulders are dotted with scars, which he deceptively blames on chickenpox, but I know better. They are permanent reminders of frantic, uncontrolled episodes of clawing oily, teenage blemishes.

"We never know where the trinket will take us." Lenny hops down. The sunlight seems to follow him, giving his hair an ice-like sheen. "With so much history in three souls, there's a lot to pick from. The jewelry box's catalog is large."

Again, Anthony only nods.

Unyielding, Lenny's broad hand caps Anthony's shoulder. "Hey." His voice is mild, candid. "Your ole man never got it."

Eyes still diverted, Anthony's quiet. Listening.

"His whole life, he lived on the outskirts," Lenny continues. "That instinct, it's in you. You're timid like your father, always one step in, then two steps back out. He had *a lot* of demons, but mostly, he was stubborn. That was his weakness. He did you wrong."

"Enough!" Olivia yells, fed up. Her vibrancy has always shaved years off her appearance, but with her strength exhausted, for the first time since I've known her, Olivia fits her age. Her cheeks droop like melting wax, pulling her lips with them, forging a prominent frown. "Leave 'em out of this. *I* took that damn box. Not them."

Dismayed, Lenny's hands find his waist. "You don't get it." He effortlessly spins the chair backward. His legs wrap the comparatively doll-sized piece of furniture, now facing Olivia. "The trinket seeks the *three* of you. You just happen to be the beneficiary."

She wipes crusted vomit from her smoker wrinkles. "The what?"

"The beneficiary. The soul most in need, but once you're found, the trinket will meet its full potential."

"If this *trinket* seeks me, well then, it can have me!" She pounds the table, sending a trickle of electricity that soaks into the wood grain. "It can try to drag *me* through this nonsense kicking and screaming, but I'll be damned if it hurts my family. The poem speaks for itself, talking about showing 'evil' and 'pain.' It will show these kids no such thing as long as I'm above ground."

"The poem simply states a truth about the human experience," Lenny argues equably. "The trips won't *all* be bad. You've had joy in your life, too. I can't tell you the trinket's purpose. Don't ask. I don't know everything. What I *can* tell you, is you'll be protected during the more difficult trips. Stop your worrying."

"What do you mean?"

"Look at your hand! Don't act like I haven't noticed. Tell me what you see?"

"A hideous growth."

He groans, exasperated.

"Take another look." Ten tightly squeezed fingers cover both eyes, impossible for light to penetrate. "That growth is the *consciousness of your soul.* It exists beyond your intellect, living inside of you. This consciousness has always been there, revealing itself in spurts, even when you've smothered it with grief. Now, the trinket has summoned it to the surface."

His fingers fan, showing the bulging whites of his eyes.

"The trinket will help you remember, it *wants* you to remember. Your soul's consciousness transformed into a shape you can understand —*an eye*—and for safety, secured itself within your palm. Your soul sees what earthly eyes cannot. It's existed long before you, and will go on after. Freed from constraints of time-bound thinking."

Olivia stands, pushing her walker aside, an exhibit of brawn. Of independence.

"I've heard this talk before," she affirms. "I'm no nitwit. You don't think I've studied the chakras? You don't think I've traveled the globe to practice the 'pathways to peace?'" Her fingers mimic quotation marks. "I know about the third eye—the mind's eye, the Ajna chakra, the eye of Horus, the atrophied pineal gland—call it what you wish, but it hasn't done me any good. I've spoken to seers, bet you didn't know that!" Her chin jerks high in provocation.

A photo hangs on the den bookshelf as proof, resting upright against an English-translated *Bhagavad Gita*. The date says February 1969, one year after the Beatles' stint in Rishikesh to practice transcendental meditation with Maharishi Mahesh Yogi. Their trip was famously productive, from a music standpoint, with John Lennon partaking in five days of mediation that helped produce material for *The White Album*. Olivia, too, wished to ruminate on ancient philosophies, and stepped foot in India wearing an embroidered over-blouse with cotton pajama trousers. Her thick American frame stood beside a svelte Indian man in a white silk dhoti. Her steely stare seemed anything but transcendent.

"I've practiced qigong so long that the balls of my feet cramped!" Olivia continues, extending her arms, wrists flexed, with one hand bent up while the other points down. Air bursts in and out of fiercely contracting nostrils. "I know people like *you*." Her finger is now a millimeter from the space between Lenny's eyes. "You find people at their weakest. You claim to have authority over the secrets of the universe, but no one does—*no one*—and I'm most fearful of those claiming they do."

Lenny doesn't react. He sits, subdued, lolling in an awkward stillness.

Finally, Olivia's shoulders cave to the weight of her arm. Her finger falls. Yet still, Lenny's *silence*.

Fifteen seconds pass. Until, eyes tightly closed with his chin raised, he begins to hum. He holds the chair's rail like the horn of a saddle as the song prompts him to sway.

His voice is trained, with full, reverberating resonance. Confidence carries his song, with a knowing that his throat is solely a vessel, and his tone a gift bestowed at birth with intention to be used. "'If you know what life is worth,'" he sings, "'you will look for yours on Earth...'"

It's a tender, lento version of a Rastafarian-inspired reggae classic: Bob Marley's "Get Up, Stand Up." I know it well as the motivation for Susanna Elwood, St. Vincent's inspiring social rights activist. She led Christian mission trips to Oaxaca, Mexico to dispense bookmarks of patron saints and proclaim the second resurrection of Jesus. "'Blessed are the poor in spirit, for theirs is the kingdom of heaven,'" she'd shout, with her Bible turned to the Gospel of Matthew in demonstration. While recruiting, she'd blare Marley's song from stereo speakers, waving pamphlets depicting the last year's charitable deeds.

I later discovered that the song was written in reaction to witnessing Haiti's impoverished communities. "I want people to live big and have enough," Marley said of the song, "so I must sing." The lyrics speak to Jamaica, a tiny country with a patchwork of religions—Catholicism, Anglicanism, Methodism, Mormonism, Islam, Judaism, Rastafarianism, and more. Marley challenged religious dissension, "sick and tired of your ism and schism game," and discouraged the acceptance of oppression by those conceding to wait for heaven in an afterlife. Not sure Susanna got that part.

Now, on the verge of tears, a knot clogs my throat. I'm taken by the piousness of his voice. There's a tingling from my nape to my tailbone. I've read the term before—Autonomous Sensory Meridian Response—or, in other words, a music orgasm, and it's appropriate. I'm overcome by elation while occupying a pew in the church of Lenny, and like a sexual orgasm, every cell screams *yes*, as if an immense, emotional pressure is releasing.

The eye upon Olivia's palm is drawn from its slumber, and upon hearing the music, transforms from teal to an incandescent magenta, gleaming like a carnival sign—*Come one, come all! Gather 'round for the show of your life!*

Lenny's crooning quiets, fading out his a cappella performance.

He opens his eyes. His pupils, now transformed to an abysmal black, connect with the eye in the palm. They share an unsaid exchange, and the energy in the room shifts. Even Olivia is docile.

"When did it happen?" he asks her.

"What do you mean?" A single tear slips. When she wipes it, she remolds the putty that is her skin.

Leaning forward, Lenny's crossed arms envelope the chair. "When did *you die?*"

Olivia goes still.

"I thought so." He smirks. "That's why the trinket found you. When a soul veers from a body, like yours did, its consciousness stirs. You're special. Only a few bear witness to the inner workings of the universe, but the beauty you witnessed was quickly masked by pain. It's not too late. The trinket is not here to harm you, Olivia. It is your *tool*."

Olivia inspects her palm, bemused. And though it's technically impossible, since the eye doesn't have a pair, I swear it winks. "I don't understand..."

Lenny retrieves the jewelry box and sets it atop the table, swiveling its base like a Lazy Susan. "It's like this. A body's weight anchors its soul to this realm, but the trinket, for a moment, *breaks* that bond. It sets your soul *free*. It flings souls across dimensions, faster than the speed of light. Souls are free to travel through the fabric of space and time." His arms spread wide, encasing Anthony and I within his invisible sphere. "The trinket has gathered its travelers. The younger souls." He nods to Anthony and me. "They're ripe. The anticipated moment you wished for, all those years ago, has come. If you want peace, you must say *yes* to this challenge."

"Why should I trust you?" Olivia glares at his hand, now resting upon mine.

He rolls his sleeve until it clears past his elbow. "You see this?" He rotates his wrist. A six-inch scar spans the length of his forearm. "It came from the noose of a lobster snare. The rope burned my flesh while my grandfather clung to its pole. For *eight minutes* he was underwater, his lifeless body swallowed by the sea. With *all* my strength I pulled him into the boat. When we drifted to land, I thought I'd be carrying a corpse."

"I'm so sorry..." I begin, but I'm stopped.

"No." His extended finger slices the air like a metronome. "My grandfather survived, but my mamma didn't make it. The waves took her. Buried her at sea. When my grandfather woke up and heard about his daughter, he was beside himself with grief. She wasn't supposed to go that day, but she begged to. To watch over me. He never talked about that day again. I was never allowed back to Pedro Bay. I was forbidden to even catch fish, but I needed work. What else could I do? I had to move."

He rolls down the sleeve and buttons the cuff, once again concealing his secret. His reminder.

"Then, one day I got a call," he continues. "It was my grandmother's voice, 'Did you send this, baby?' she says. 'Nah, ma'am,' I says, 'wasn't me.' She spoke of the trinket. It was delivered to my grandfather with no return address. I had this urge. I decided I must visit him, I must go back to Jamaica, so I did. That's when it happened. The trinket took us back to the sea. Through my grandfather's eyes, it made me understand. It *showed* me what he saw that day. The day he almost died." He leans forward, closing the gap between them. "You know what I'm talking about, Olivia. You just need a reminder, like he did. You said you cannot trust those claiming to have the answers. So, why don't you see for yourself?"

Aunt Olivia looks to me. Not for help, she doesn't want that, but for assurance. She needs to know she's doing the right thing. I know Olivia. Her well-being is not her concern. "And what if I say yes?"

Lenny smiles. "Then you're goin' to need these."

From his pocket of treasures he pulls two more: a wooden coaster and a Motorola two-way pager.

"What the hell are we supposed to do with that?" Anthony snatches the pager. It's archaic. There's a crack in the plastic case and it's missing the space bar.

Lenny's signature laugh echoes against the walls. "This is from your guide. Pagers use a simpler radio frequency. Cellular frequencies will hamper her senses. She'll need her faculties intact."

"Our guide? You're not coming?" Olivia cries, but the news is a shock to us all.

"Like I say, don't fear. You're in good hands. I'm just standing in. She will tell you much more than I can." Lenny takes the pager from Anthony and sets the items before the jewelry box. "Listen to this." Head tilted, his stare strong,he scans the table and demands our attention, one by one. "You will embark on seven journeys. With three already complete, only four remain. The trinket won't stop 'til it returns to the location where your soul's consciousness was first rattled. Go there soon. Don't waste no time. The trinket will not wait. Then, after the fifth trip, use this." He aligns the coaster upon the palm's eye like a sleep mask.

Olivia's entire body relaxes with a sigh of relief. "It's like Icy Hot."

"It is made from pure olivewood," he explains. "It acts like an insulator, trapping the electric current. It gives you time, 'til your guide finds you, but you must hold it steady. If the electrons can exit, they will gather and form a bigger, stronger current stream, and the pain will be, well, excruciating."

"Noted." Olivia gently removes the coaster, treating it like the royal jewels. "Why wait for the fifth trip?"

"'Cause after the fifth trip the earthly senses are exhausted—sight, smell, hearing, touch, taste. That means you'll be exhausted. But the third eye has powers beyond this Earth. Its strength far exceeds *you*, but your guide is seasoned. Her abilities will aid yours, which leads me to this." He shuffles the pager with his fingers. "It's a two-way, and only one number is saved in the address book: *Meira*. She'll be your guide."

"Who is she?" I ask. I know no one by that name.

He thinks it over, biting his knuckle. "You will see," he decides. "She's hard to explain, but you'll know soon enough. Just be sure to page her with the *exact* location of where you are in the journey. She will meet you. Without her, dawg nyam yuh suppa."

"Huh?" We exchange looks, lost.

Lenny laughs, leaning forward. “It won’t be good.”

With a pop, the jewelry box leaps into the air, then slowly descends. The opal gemstones transform into an iridescent, warping base of black, with specks of midnight blues and fiery reds that create a galaxy, a portal with wildly spitting lightning bolts.

“That’s my cue.” He stands, towering over the table. His robust mane eclipses the light fixture, casting a shadow on the jewelry box.

He walks toward the door before we can contest. Anthony shoots me a stare. Translation: *Get him*. I follow behind, picking up speed to beat him to the entrance.

“Wait!” Arms spread, I block the door. “You can’t leave us. Olivia’s old, and scared—scratch that, Anthony and I are scared—we can’t do it without you. What if we mess up? Olivia already doesn’t trust you, or anyone, and—”

His hand cups my mouth. It’s moist from perspiration; beads of sweat seep between my lips, tasting of salt, and *the sea;* his past, ingrained into his being. Sniffing the trapped air takes me to the shore, slightly sulfury with a briny finish.

“Understand this,” he explains. “I’ve had my turn. I was like you once, but my time-traveling days are done. But Meira, now, she is the *real* traveler.”

With flat palms, he presses his hands together, in prayer position. “Believe it or not, I can relate to Olivia. I’m ready for what comes next, not what has passed.” He reaches around me for the knob.

“Plus, I have to get back.” He nods to the car window, rolled down for ventilation. The beads slung over the mirror sway, coyly taping the stacked papers, nudged by a transient breeze taunting its powers, capable of scattering the pile with one, tenacious gust. “Those assignments can’t grade themselves.”

“You’re a teacher?”

“I’m many things.” He rubs his hands, creating friction. “I’m an entertainer, most of all, but I teach music as a side gig. It’s good for the kids. They enjoy it, and truthfully, so do I.”

From endless pockets he acquires a harmonica, and with a deep breath, skillfully plays a C major scale.

"I'm tough," he boasts, one eyebrow raised. "With me, the kids learn the basics. They don't want to, *at first*. They come to me trying to sing like pop stars, but I make them *read* the music. That's the part that takes skill, and time."

The top paper rustles, flashing an exaggeratingly large D+. He wasn't kidding.

Sunlight catches a metal latch. In the back seat, what I'd assumed were empty boxes are cases for instruments. One, round and fat, like an oversized hatbox—a bass drum. Beside it, a lean handle that voluptuously thickens at the bottom—a guitar, whose strings are surely the culprit of his toughened fingertips that now twist the doorknob.

"Wait!"

He sighs.

"Why did you choose to be a Rastafarian?"

"A Rasta-man?" His head cocks back, genuinely alarmed at the assumption. "What makes you say that?" A single dreadlock dislodges from the cove of his ear, grazing his cheek.

"I see. It's the hair, isn't it?" He smirks, seemingly enjoying, and aware, that he's in control of his image, yet possesses the secret that there's more than what meets the eye. "You got me confused. It's a good look!"

I point to the lion of Judah thread onto the beads, cemented in a liberating roar. "What about that? It's part of the culture, no?"

He spots the charm in question. "Ah, of course. That was my mother's. Rastafarians have a long history, starting in the 1930s. She was involved in its beginnings. I was raised with the teachings, but like you, I challenge what I'm told. I keep the beads because they remind me of her, and the traditions she lived, and gave to me. Why must I abandon those? Yes, I discovered *my own* way, but I have not forgotten the starting point of my path."

"Those beliefs must still resonate with you. Like the song you sang," I point out. "Bob Marley was famous for his Rastafarian beliefs."

He pauses, and thinks for a moment. "Sure." Nodding in agreement. "But June, you ask too many questions. Sometimes you mustn't think too hard about those things. Just enjoy the music."

His arms spread wide to showcase his exposed chest, the V of his collar baring the skin above his heart. Holding posture, he pivots toward the car of brimming, mish-mashed enterprises. "Like I said, I do many things! I teach, I perform, I promote, I dance..." His snaps his fingers to the beat of nimble hips. "But at my core, I'm still an entertainer. If you want a successful career, you must adapt. You must be *open* to possibilities."

With a giant step he's past my bodily barricade and halfway outside, humming a tune I do not recognize. A tune all his own.

"One last question!" I ask. He pauses, but stays facing forward. "Did it work? Does your grandfather have his peace?"

I can't see it, but I sense his smile. "Yes." In unison, his shoulders drop. His face finds, and feels, the sun. "He has his peace."

Still parked out front is the Ford Taurus: his ride home. About where the sidewalk ends, he stops. Again, he shuffles through his pocket. What he finds is too tiny for me to see, but when the light catches the sparkling silver I know—his earrings. He tosses them in the air like dice, and with his free hand, gives a peace sign.

"Don't forget!" he yells. "Always stretch toward the light!" With that, he hops in the driver's seat. Windows down as he takes off, the radio waves linger like dust, and Johnny Nash's voice rings out, "*Gone are the dark clouds that had me blind...*"

He takes a left at the four-way stop, bound for Cleveland.

Succumbing to fatigue, I brace my forehead against the door. The oil from my pores polishes the wood.

What are we getting into? My head is spinning.

Here's what I know: *time travel.* Literature feeds the imagination with the possibility of revisiting the past, and poses the question, "What if?"

What if Hitler was killed before World War II, what if we met our parents before we were born, what if we hadn't taken that train, or answered that call, or squashed that butterfly with the rubber soles of our hiking boots, irreplaceably altering future events.

As dreamy as it sounds, a physicist understands this is a fantasy. As an object travels faster it gets heavier, making it harder to achieve acceleration. Then there's the grandfather paradox, which suggests that even if we *could* go back in time, we'd put the relationship of cause and effect at odds—if a man made an irreversible error, like married his mother before his father had the chance, he wouldn't be alive to attempt to time travel in the first place.

But these stories focus on the living, with the weighted baggage of limbs, organs, and skin, and the ability to warp space with a body's mass. What they don't ask is what happens when an intangible contender challenges light? A contender with zero mass that is physically unable to manipulate a past action, like flirt with their mom, but can still slip into an alternate dimension. What if Lenny is correct? What if, when our soul is granted the opportunity to escape the burdening weight of our body, it can race against light, *and win*?

"June!" It's Olivia.

I sprint back, remembering that the jewelry box had been active before Lenny's farewell, but when I return, Olivia appears tranquil, as does the jewelry box. It was a false alarm. She licks her fingers to smooth the flyaway hairs charged by electricity. Winston has returned and curled at her feet, with pointed hairs that turn his torso into a pincushion.

"We must say yes," she declares.

It's unexpected. What *was* expected was a fight; at least a conversation, but she appears resolute.

Grinding metal shrills as Olivia opens the storage drawer below the oven. Finding a baking mitt, she shields the eye, now closed, from the outside world.

"There's just one thing," she says, locking her eyes with mine. "For me to feel OK with this, I need to know that whatever should happen, *you* will be OK."

She pulls the jewelry box close and rubs each opal like a rabbit's foot, hoping for luck.

I look to Anthony. His eyes meet mine. Together, an unspoken decision is made.

"Aunt Ol, no matter what happens, our reality has already changed. We say yes."

"Go get dressed," she orders. "We're going to Hamtramck."

11

OLIVIA, EIGHTY-EIGHT YEARS OLD (PRESENT TIME)

"It just needs a minute to charge, then I'm ready to go." June plugs her phone into the outlet. She's changed into jeans and a t-shirt that swallows her whole. She knots the extra cloth behind her back, baring protruding hip bones.

Picking through a stash of plastic grocery bags I find two without rips, then double-bag the jewelry box for a sturdy hold. June found me a winter mitten in the coat closet, baby blue with a cross-stitch snowflake. The oven mitt would've been practical, for flame retardant and safety reasons, but this one's more subtle. At least I look less like the Hamburger Helper mascot.

This isn't my first pilgrimage. In my forties, I embarked on the Pilgrims' Way, the route immortalized in Chaucer's *Canterbury Tales*. Starting in Winchester, England, the hundred-and-twenty-mile hike winds through a causeway dating back to the Stone Age, ruthlessly testing my stamina and blistering my toes. The end goal, the Canterbury Cathedral, stewards the shrine of Thomas Becket, a slain twelfth-century Catholic archbishop once at odds with King Henry II. But, despite the scandalous history, he did not spark my interest. I much preferred the tale of the Wife of Bath.

Chaucer's fictitious female widower held staunch aspirations for sovereignty over her five husbands: "*But sith I hadde hem hoolly in myn hond*," she brags. She is bold for the era—a bullheaded feminist who challenges society's preference for a woman who is obedient and chaste. Though she is flawed—aggression and hypocrisy being two unsavory traits—her proclamation to being her own authority results in a life of her choosing.

I sought the lands that inspired such a character, in all of her complexity. And now, years later, I channel her fortitude and accept Lenny's challenge to be my own authority through experience. I'd be daft to ignore that, from a spiritual standpoint, the Wife of Bath did not seem to progress, even ending her tale with spite (specifically, requesting that Jesus shorten the lives of men who govern their wives). But I'm choosing not to dwell on that part. Nobody's perfect, right?

I'm seated at the kitchen window. Anthony's outside, cleaning the van by shoving grease-stained McDonald's wrappers into the trunk. Lenny's words echo as I watch: "*The trinket seeks the three of you*," and if I'm being honest, he was right. Anthony is the true reason I agreed to this pursuit.

Each trip turns me into an empath, taking on the emotions of fellow travelers. With June, I sense curiosity—openness to possibility and excitement for where the race leads. But with Anthony, I'm overwhelmed by darkness, even in the presence of this magnificent light, as if it was not meant for me, and never will be. The light is simply a tease, judging me unworthy. It's awful.

When we returned from Anthony's trip, a great ache tore through my bones. I now *see* how much desperation and anger is in his soul.

"Ready!" Anthony yells, brushing trans-fat residue off his fingertips.

June insists I take the front seat while she slides into the back. Anthony retrieves a mangled GPS from the glovebox, but I push it aside.

"If I'm the designated navigator you'll have to trust me."

"Fine. Where to?" he asks, sharply.

"My childhood home."

His face drops, realizing our destination, and more specifically, the reason.

"Go to where your soul's consciousness was first rattled," Lenny advised. As it turns out, Anthony relived the last moment he saw his father alive, and I will too.

"I don't need a map," I assure him. "Take I-94, it's the quickest."

He does as he's told. We sit quietly as Anthony pulls onto the eastbound ramp to Detroit.

June breaks the silence. "Are you nervous, Aunt Ol?"

She occupies the bucket seat behind mine. Her smudged reflection shows in my passenger side window.

I could answer truthfully—*I'm scared shitless*—or I could pretend to be the wise old aunt.

"Terrified," I say. She accepts the answer without further questioning. Exhausted, we all let silence take over.

The white noise of the highway numbs us until Anthony fumbles with the radio dials and lends our ears to the DJ instead, but no one's really listening. We need time to entertain trepidations.

The rationale for this mission doesn't sit right with me. How can reliving suffering bring peace? After all, isn't the whole point of psychotherapy, my ninety-dollar- per-hour weekly indulgence, to vanquish the bullshit that haunts me? To conquer problematic behaviors and develop coping mechanisms when uncontrolled triggers, like tormenting, sporadic flashbacks arise?

Sure, life is suffering. That's what Buddha said. The imperfection of human nature gives in to the inevitability that suffering will be experienced. I don't recall "dwell on the past" in Buddha's footnotes.

In 1975 I found myself in Kanazawa, Japan, seeking enlightenment at a monastery. It took a good amount of tries, all while uncomfortably perched on folded knees, but I eventually meditated my way to a spiritual awakening. There, surrounded by monks of the Daijoji Temple, I harnessed the energy of grace and benevolence, that which inspired the Buddha and Bodhisattvas, and released my mind from earthly desires.

Since then, I've managed to quell my wants—designer handbags, cable television, money, power, even the thought of welcoming another spring or summer—they've all dulled, that is, except one: the desire to see my loved ones again.

It is because of this desire, that in my heart of hearts, I could not embrace the Buddhist teachings, not wholly, and instead have held onto a prominent principle of Catholicism that gives me comfort: the notion of a heaven.

I've ripped the Bible once in my life. I was sixteen. The severed page was stashed under my mattress. I prayed the words would infiltrate my mind as I slept, an attempt at subliminal learning, and a superstition that if I willed it, the words would come true. The page in question was Luke 13:29–30—"*People will come from east and west and north and south, and will take their places at the feast in the kingdom of God. Indeed there are those who are last who will be first, and first who will be last.*"

I've never believed in heaven in the traditional sense. I did not imagine an old man with a long, burly beard trolling the pearly gates with a shepherd's staff. But I ached for a seat at that table. I've held on to the hope I'll see my loved ones again. That I'll crawl onto my father's lap as he reads the *Free Press*, or hug my mother's ankles as she powders her nose, or sing my baby to sleep, *just one more time*. I'll be reunited with them in the form I once knew.

Their images are etched in my memory; I've imprinted their touch on my skin, and though idealistic, this is unsubstantial. My faith has been adulterated. Heaven may not be what awaits my departed soul, at least not in the construct I've envisioned. I must let that hope go.

Now, seated on the passenger side of Anthony's van, I caress the wooden coaster in the gusset pocket of my purse and silently make a resolution: that until it knocks me senseless, I will endure the pain. If the jewelry box is determined to teach me a lesson through suffering, well then, *bring it on.*

As if on cue, a tingling sensation rolls down my forearm like a pinched nerve. It tightens, clawing my hand by contracting my tendons. Fine lashes brush against the inside of the mitten.

The eye is awake.

12

JUNE, TWENTY-EIGHT YEARS OLD (PRESENT TIME)

I've envisioned myself in the back seat of a van with Anthony behind the wheel, but with the purpose of calming a baby in the car seat. To be here with an obese cat and his fast food mess is downright depressing.

We were waiting to have kids. Excuses accumulated whenever the topic was brought up. Now I regret it. Though our marriage dissolved I'd at least have a child in this lifetime. God, that sounds selfish, but then again, I'll argue otherwise.

My mom consoled me: "You dodged a bullet!" I appreciated her trying to cheer me up, but the argument that a married couple is necessary for a stable childhood pisses me off. Kids are born into far worse conditions every minute. One doting parent is more than many get, and I can't help but take offense to the unintentional undermining of my ability to provide a loving home.

"June!" Olivia shrieks. Winston's leaping through a slim opening in the back-seat window. He's midair into oncoming traffic. "Grab the cat!" He miraculously dodges vehicles in a high-stakes game of *Frogger* and scuttles through an open field. "Pull over!"

With a jerk of the wheel, Anthony takes the next exit. The van veers off the highway. Anthony rolls to a complete stop and I lunge from the van's sliding door, completing two full somersaults and standing to see grass-stain streaked shins.

Winston's stubby legs aren't slowing down. He's a plus-sized Furby on speed. Detroit is known for vacant lots, and the further he runs, the taller the weeds grow.

I haven't been to the gym in years and it shows. My chest hurts from my heart working overtime to supply nutrients to my lungs, nutrients that I rarely replenish thanks to a festering binge-purge habit. I'm cramping. My legs can't keep up; their jelly consistency's unfit for sustained running. I crawl to a halt and cover my face in bitter defeat. "Damn it, Winnie."

A large, firm hand lands on my shoulder. "Where'd he go?" It's Anthony, who is equally out of breath.

"Straight ahead." I point toward the massive industrial wonderland that sprawls before us. "He's heading north, toward the General Motors Assembly Plant."

"What do we do?" Anthony slashes the tall grass with karate moves. Winston's out of sight.

Olivia's scratchy voice yells from the parked van. "Why are you wasting time on foot when we have a car? *Vamos*!" She has a point. We jog back to the car, hands on hips, sucking in air.

Olivia takes control. "Turn onto East Grand Boulevard until it becomes Hamtramck Drive. We'll circle the perimeter of the plant. "The cat isn't in any better shape than the two of you. He'll tucker out eventually." She studies the discolored map she found in the console, the streets dotted with bleeding red and blue road markers from old water-spills.

"Winston! Winston!" Anthony is a lunatic screaming for a cat who hasn't answered to his name since the day we brought him home, but I appreciate the effort. We're driving at a snail's pace, pissing off the cars behind us who honk with disapproval. A truck speeds around us. "Move it, Grandma!"

Olivia, quite jovially, uses her good hand to flip him the bird.

A chain link fence guards the plant, making it impossible to explore without access to enter the grounds. When we reach Joseph Campau Street, Olivia makes a split-second decision. "Take a left!" Anthony swerves, cutting off an approaching Buick. My life flashes before my eyes.

I breathe a sigh of relief, but something's wrong with Olivia. Her shoulders furiously tremor as sweat pours down her jawline.

"Is she having a seizure?" Anthony yells, slapping her cheek while trying to maintain control of the wheel. "Where'd she put that coaster?"

"I don't know. I know she took it, but I lost track after that." I double check for the pager in my pocket. We were instructed to wait until the fifth trip, but the hell with it. If needed, I'm messaging this Meira, ready or not.

"Olivia!" I crawl over the console and straddle her waist. Unlike earlier, when the palm's eye appeared, she's losing consciousness. The jewelry box, still encased within the plastic bag, is placid. Her two eyes roll behind her lids, whereas before, her senses were heightened. I know these symptoms. They are not the jewelry box's doing.

"Did she eat before we left?" I ask Anthony, frantic.

"How am I supposed to know? I don't feed her."

"She's diabetic. She's hypoglycemic. We need to get her food. NOW." I lean out the window to scan our surroundings. A two-story brick building with striped green and white awnings sits on the corner of Holbrook and Dubois. A framed, wooden door tucked into an all-glass storefront welcomes its patrons to Café Ardenne.

"There! The café. I'll run in."

I hurl the door open, nearly sending the hanging bell airborne, and then stumble over the uneven antique oak floors. "Shit!" I scream, but fight through the stubbed toe's pain.

The barista is a vintage-wearing hipster with a beard that brushes his buttoned-up collar. A fitted plaid shirt balances his cuffed, dark-wash jeans like an aesthetic mullet—outdoorsy on top and metropolitan on the bottom. His deer-in-headlights expression tells me he's terrified of the unhinged girl scrambling toward the counter.

"Orange juice!" I demand. "Or sugar. Anything!"

He nods. "Sure thing." Then he lobs a rectangular plastic holder filled with sugar packets. I make a white-knuckle catch and rush past the latte-sipping patrons back onto the bleak street. He doesn't question my motive, and I'm thankful. His energy is kind, almost magnetic. I almost look back, but there's no time.

I spot Anthony's upper body teetering out of the driver-seat window.

"Hurry!" he yells.

An oncoming Cadillac approaches. I calculate if I can sprint across but decide against it.

"*Come on, come on, come on...*" Angst shakes my knees. I'm ready to run the instant the coast is clear. As the car passes, a mixture of dirt and rainwater splashes onto my jeans. "For fuck's sake!" I instinctively glance down to assess the filth, and when I look up, a brilliant white beam shoots from the van toward the pale blue sky.

Blinded, Anthony loses his balance and crashes onto the cracked asphalt. I clench his shirt to help him up. Together we peek into the van to find Olivia's frozen body. She's racing the light.

13

OLIVIA, TWENTY-FIVE YEARS OLD (SIXTY-THREE YEARS AGO)

Smoke billows from the plant's chimneys, a sign of economic prosperity for the family homes bordering the industrial fortress. Food will be on the table at dinner, maybe a new Ford automobile in the driveway. One day the whole gang will relocate to the suburbs, upgrade to a bigger house surrounded by shopping centers and land to roam. The American Dream is thirty miles outside of the city, but for now, they'll forfeit the sunlight to get the job done.

I admire the view from a curb on Hamtramck Drive. My flat-tired bicycle is like dead carcass on the side of the road. I rode the rims until they bent from my weight; now I'm kicking dirt around, lighting up a cigarette until the ambition comes to walk for help. It's four o'clock. It's hot. First-shifters will be released soon. If I hold my thumb up when a motorist nears, surely a taker will heed my plea.

The shelves of DeVinke and Co are stocked with an amount of nuts sufficient to prepare a squirrel for winter. Salted, boiled, roasted, dipped in chocolate, all the fancy kinds that sell for the reasonable price of an arm and a leg. Janie Stevens is three months older than me but two steps higher on the corporate ladder. She let me go ahead of schedule for good behavior, and what do I do with the extra time? Roast *myself* in the summer heat.

A shiny Buick Super Wagon speeds around the curve, wood paneling and ruby-red hood. The ankle-deep potholes and poor shocks send it bouncing up and down.

"Hey! Hey buddy!" I holler, chasing the bumper. My worn-out, strappy sandals smack the pavement, a pair of Sonnets that fit every occasion but are at the end of their rope.

A young woman, early twenties, with a bouncy blond brushed-under bob and a back seat stuffed with kids and groceries is driving. She didn't bat an eye at the girl maniacally waving with a cig dangling from her lip. But in this scenario, I'm not the girl. I'm twenty-five years old. By the looks of it, I have five years on her. Five years to have matured, to have made something of myself, to have contributed to society. She's juggling responsibilities and feeding hungry mouths, and me, well, I'm stuck on the side of the road coming home from a job that pays the rent and my bar tabs with little to spare.

A group of fellas exit the plant in navy blue jumpsuits. The placement of grease streaks is the only unique identifier, like stripes on a zebra. They're an army marching out, but the crowds are silent, the streets are empty. Their work ethic deserves notoriety, but instead they'll remain the common man, nameless to the society who functions on everything they touch.

Mary Janes pitter-patter in the distance, medium-heeled, made for comfort. A purse slapping a hip on the downswing adds to the layers of sound. Next is heavy breathing, broken by the sound of something snapping and a loud, exasperated groan.

I spin around to spot an older woman, I would guess around fifty, wearing a pale blue uniform topped off with a large white collar, like one of those contraptions placed around the necks of dogs after surgery. Her grayish brown hair is tousled into a French twist, with a few loose strands that have escaped the bobby pins' hold.

"Join the club." I offer a cigarette with my thumb on the wheel of the lighter, ready to ignite. We're two working chicks with bum transportation. She's down to one heel and I'm stuck with one wheel.

"Thanks, sweetie."

My dad used to call me sweetie. I immediately take to her.

"Whatchu doin' on the side of the road?"

"I'm guessing the same thing you are, except coming from work, not going." She hasn't looked at me since sitting down; I could have three heads and a pistol but it doesn't faze her. She just stares off at the smoky plant as the ants go marching one by one.

"I'd say I'm tardy, but it'll likely be AWOL. My ass doesn't need another grabbing. The boys can open their own damn beers." She finishes the cigarette in a record number of drags and smashes it against the curb. "Thanks, sweetie."

"You *inhaled* that." I'm both appalled and impressed. There's a quality that's not right about her. She's physically here but mentally disconnected, in another world, a safer one constructed after this one let her down. Since she's showing no interest in my appearance, I take the opportunity to examine hers. She's no spring chicken but seems too young to have liver spots; yet, they mottle her neck and distract from her face, which, aside from the multitude of wrinkles, is pleasant. Her nose is petite, her cheekbones high, and her eyebrows arch to frame her hazel eyes. Her cleavage hides under that hideous oversized white collar, but the shape of her shoulders hints that she'd look lovely in a boat-necked blouse. Her nylons have rips along the hem and should have been thrown out months ago.

"What's the point of stockings if they only cover half your leg?" I jab to ease the tension. I peg her as the sort of lady who can take it and give it back without flinching.

"Mind your own beeswax. You want to buy a new pair for me?"

I've made her self-conscious. She flaps her skirt, smoothing the kinks and sending dust airborne. She stretches the hemline to veil a kneecap peeking through a fist-sized hole. As she does, a red and purple bruise makes a brief appearance on her right thigh, the clear outline of a large hand double the size of her own. I can't unsee what I saw. "Woah! What is that?" I grab for her skirt but she slaps my hand.

"What the hell was that for?" I try to rub out the sting.

"Sorry, kid. I didn't hurt ya, did I?" She's embarrassed. She goes quiet. It's clear she's not concerned about the slap anymore. I'm fine. She contemplates if she wants to divulge grittier details to a complete stranger. An unbiased third party, someone she will never see again, can be the perfect keeper of a dirty little secret. The random traveler who shares a row on the bus, the shopper next in line at a checkout, the fellow patient waiting at the doctor's office; all may learn juicier, more honest details than the person we go home to. I wait.

"I shouldn't have reacted that way. I didn't mean it." She stands to pace, and then cracks her knuckles and flicks her wrists like she's shaking them dry. "Do you know why a woman would stay when her fella beats her?" she blurts, her truth coming to surface.

How do I respond? I haven't a clue. My father deeply loved my mother and only raised his hand to signal for another helping of mashed potatoes. Then there's me. I live by my own rules, free of the need to ask permission from a man, or woman for that matter. Why anyone would stay in a situation that causes pain is beyond me.

"Because there's unfinished business. There's an avenue that hasn't been exhausted. There's more to give. There's a glimmer of hope that he'll straighten up, find his way, treat ya right. So, you take the beating and let his foul words cut deeper than his belt and pray for the best. As much as you want to kill that son-of-a-bitch, that son-of-a bitch is your only ally."

Her outfit is tattered beyond the torn stockings. The belt that cinches her dress is fastened with a safety pin, and her waist, it's tinier than a baby doll's. No doubt she lives on nicotine and the grace of God.

"Do you need money?" I pop open my double clasp coin purse, scrambling for the right amount of change that could place her on the next bus to anywhere.

She starts laughing at the sight. "Darling, put your money away. I'm not rich but I could leave if I wanted to. I doubt he'd use his energy to chase me, he'd be too liquored-up on vodka to navigate from the sofa." The heat's relentless. Sweat droplets contour her hairline, a tiara when the sun hits at the perfect angle.

"You meet someone who cares for you, would do anything for you, and you think, 'Hell, I'm finally gettin' a piece of the pie.' Then he starts smacking you sidewise while saying 'I love you,' and you realize he's no better than the rest of 'em. I leave this one and the next will be the same man in another fat, inebriated form, so why bother? At least I know how this one works. It's like living in a warzone, honey. I survive because I know the streets to avoid and the times to go inside. I got myself, and that's more than most."

She retakes her seat on the warm cement. "Do you believe in reincarnation, honey?" It's an unexpected query from a woman whose crucifix pendant peaks through the opening between her shirt buttons. "I've been thinking about it a lot lately. Maybe those eastern cultures are onto something. Everything else goes in cycles, right? Famine, war, riches, fashion. Why can't I? I want another shot at this."

Her eyes hold her pain, vulnerability shining through hazel irises. Deep pools of color carry the weight of lifetimes past. She's due for a change.

"I figure the good Lord didn't deal a decent hand for me this round because he was strategizing for a real winner when my turn comes again. You know, I'll be born into a family that drinks tea and eats crumpets, real fancy-like, the lovey-dovey kind. We'll take cruises in the Caribbean to escape winters, and maybe I'll find a nice gent and be real gone. Won't stop thinking about him, and he'll be hooked on me, too. He'll treat me right. Can you imagine, doll? You know. That'd be real nice."

"What do we got here?" A new string of men exit the plant, virtually identical to the gang that just left, same grease-streaked jumpsuits and pomade-lathered manes, messed from hours of wiping the sweat from their brows. Whistles and catcalls commence. "Heya, Dolly, let's get a drink!" They're heading in our direction. They're collectively young, about mid-twenties. That's the age that stays after quitting time because they're not yet dragged down by the monotony of the work; they're still trying to prove their worth, and the freedom of bachelorhood provides the flexibility to arrive home when they please without a riled wife waiting with a meal gone cold.

There are six men total, walking two by two like Bemelmans's cutesy *Madeline* drawing. The thought's entertaining:

In a grease-pit in Detroit,

That was covered in grime,

Walked six tired men,

In two straight lines.

And just like the children's book, occupying the caboose is a head covered with lush auburn ringlets, a shiny ball of fire bringing up the rear, trailing a row of greasers. He's a break from the norm, a looker with a straight frame and soft smile. "Keep up, Jacoby!" the leader calls. "The first round's on me!" With that, he picks up the pace.

"Hooligans, all of them." My friend's not enticed by the offer. She catches my googly eyes for the lone redhead, and her slender elbow nudges my ribcage. "Go on, bug off. Have fun. I could be their mother. But be careful, will ya? And how about a smoke before ya go?"

I hand her a fresh cig, my last one, then place my hand on her knee, making contact with the skin peeking through the nylon's hole as she reaches for her lighter. "I hope you get your wish."

She's confused. "Huh?"

"Your wish. I hope the next life treats you right." The sun's rays reflect off her metallic lighter and spotlight a shiny penny resting between the curb and her Mary Janes.

"Penny for your thoughts?" I joke, then pick it up and offer it to her.

"I normally don't take handouts, but eh, why not. I could use a bit of luck." She places the coin snuggly into the pocket of her A-line skirt.

"I never got your name?" I ask, standing to meet the fellas.

"Mae. Short and sweet."

"Hop in line, pretty lady!" The man in the front of the pack is the ringleader. He acts like Brando but looks like Rooney, and his confidence, and lack of self-awareness for his physical shortcomings, makes him inexplicably attractive. The top two buttons of his uniform are undone to let air filter through, exposing a stocky, barrel chest with a patch of whiskers. He's no taller than 5'6" but walks on his tiptoes with a bounce, granting him another inch with every step. I do as he says and hop in line, in the back of the line, next to a timidly tall drink of water that hasn't yet said two words.

The redhead nods. I purse my lips and flash a smile. He scratches at the ring of dirt circling his neck, I smooth a strand of hair behind my ear, and together we walk side-by-side.

The clouds spread, handing over the sky to the afternoon sun. The rays bounce off the black asphalt, causing eyes to squint and heads to turn away, stealthily transporting my soul to its former realm.

14

ANTHONY, TWENTY-EIGHT YEARS OLD (PRESENT TIME)

"What are you doing!?" June flings soiled Kleenex and crushed peppermints from Olivia's purse. She's frantic.

"I'm checking her blood sugar to know how many packets to use. She'll be awake any minute. We need to make sure her body's alive when her soul returns."

June recovers a plastic, pen-shaped cylinder and presses it against the tip of Olivia's index finger, steering clear of the palm's eye, which anchors the electric current between its pupil and the jewelry box peeking through a double-knotted grocery bag. She punctures skin. Blood gathers into a shiny, miniscule ball.

"Hold this." The pen hits my chest and bounces onto my thigh.

"You could have stabbed me! This can't be sanitary." I quickly set it on the dashboard's ledge. June remains focused.

Olivia's blood seeps onto a flimsy strip of paper, which June inserts into a machine that resembles a Tamagotchi she had in middle school. She never could keep her pet alive. She rarely fed it, always ignored it, and the poop symbols piled up. Let's hope she's better with elderly humans.

"I knew it. She's at forty-five." She rips open three sugar packets and pries Olivia's jaw open. The white powder sticks to her dry lips and nostrils like snorted cocaine. June shoves her fingers into Olivia's mouth, pushing sugar to the back of her throat.

"Use this." I punch the glove compartment and it drops onto Olivia's knees. A half-empty water bottle rolls out, knocking the illuminated jewelry box, glowing with the now familiar, yet still hauntingly alluring blues and teals. The bottle's contact with the box breaks the current's flow, and like the flick of a switch, the light disappears.

Olivia's chest abruptly extends as she gasps for air, popping a button from her blouse that causes a bull's-eye crack on my windshield.

"Breathe, Olly, breathe." June supports her neck to prevent her from choking. Olivia erupts into a coughing fit, and the sugar water splatters onto the van door. June quickly rips open a new packet to replace the nutrients lost, then maternally combs Olivia's hair with her fingers. "Are you with us?"

Olivia twists around, confused with her surroundings. "Where am I?" Her clenched hand relaxes. A penny, blackened with grime, slips into a crevice in the floor mat. The jewelry box's delivery.

June sees I'm terrified, fidgeting, and unsure of how to help. "She'll come to. Just give her a minute," she assures, massaging her great-aunt's shoulders. "Once she's stable, we need to get her into the café. The sugar will bring her serum glucose level up, but it will drop again if we don't get her something more substantial."

"It all happened so quickly," I recall. "You were gone, what, five minutes? Her shaking got worse, then she went ballistic and ripped the mitten off, like she was possessed. That's when you came outside from the café, but before I could do anything the jewelry box lit up like a Christmas tree and my ass was on the pavement."

Olivia's alert now, taking sips of water without assistance.

"No one's blaming you, Anthony. It's obvious the jewelry box does what it wants, when it wants." June checks Olivia for a pulse. "Her heart rate's coming down. Here. Help me out. Open the van door and we'll get her inside. Careful now."

We each take a side and support Olivia's way through the glass door and into the café.

"You're back!" The barista tucks his washcloth into his belt loop and rushes to June, but halts when he catches sight of Olivia. "Woah! Oh shit, wow, ah, do you need an ambulance?" He back-pedals toward the counter while reaching into his pocket for his cell phone. Typical. The dude reeks of urban pretentiousness and cheap beard wax. No doubt he spends hours procuring obscure coffee and fixing bicycles, like every other entitled, trust-fund baby gentrifying the city who lifts their nose to Bud Light.

"A chair will do." I catch June smiling. "Her blood sugar dropped, but it's under control."

"What kind of food do you serve here..." I interject, then spot his nametag, "Mikey?" I widen my shoulders and straighten my posture. I could care less if I sound like a condescending ass. I don't like his vibe, it's too focused on June.

June cuts in. "A sandwich would be great, thanks. Something with protein. Peanut butter or a deli meat."

"Turkey and ham?"

"Perfect," June responds, then reprimands me in a harsh whisper. "Cool it, Anth. He's been a huge help. Now, take Olivia's arm. We'll lower her into a chair."

Mikey returns with a plastic-wrapped double-decker sandwich and an apple-flavored juice box. The meat's stacked an inch thick, with layers of bean sprouts and tomatoes. I'm starving.

"On the house," he offers. I'm tempted to bargain for another.

The bell rings and a young couple walk in. Their child is strapped to the father's chest, cheeks smushed and feet flapping. I glance around the tiny café. It's packed. Aside from the teenage boy with headphones the size of hamburgers, all eyes are on us.

"Nothing to see here!" I yell, uncomfortable with the attention. They return to their books and conversations, now and then suspiciously sneaking glimpses.

June slips the glove back on to shield the palm's eye. The jewelry box is left in the car. We didn't want to leave it alone, but it's too risky to bring inside. Olivia nibbles on the sandwich, dazed.

"I saw him," Olivia mumbles.

I turn to June. She shrugs her shoulders.

"Saw who?" June asks, leaning closer. "Do you mean you saw someone during your trip?"

Olivia takes a hardier bite, then nods to the large glass window facing Holbrook, crumbs spilling onto her blouse. "I saw *him*."

On the coffee shop's patio, an old man has his back to us, sitting crossed-legged in a forest-green plastic garden chair, reading the *Detroit News*. He wears a flat, woolen cap that seems unbearable in this summer heat, which oddly goes with his long-sleeved button-down shirt.

He sips his espresso. The side of his face comes into view, a bubbled nose that sneezed a mustache and white caterpillar eyebrows that support the lid of his cap. Underneath all that hair is a rosy complexion flushed from caffeine.

Without warning, a black-and-brown-marbled cat pounces onto the stool where the man's drink rests, purring for a neck scratching.

"Winston!" I stand to make sure. June joins, on her tiptoes. I can't believe it. We wasted twenty minutes on a damn cat that doesn't give the slightest indication he's worried about the family he left behind.

The old man messes the fur atop Winston's head, then scratches under his double chins. He finishes the last sip of coffee, refolds the newspaper, and extends his arms into the air for a deep, lumbering stretch, then heads for the door. Olivia watches intently.

"Well, shit." She punctures the juice box with the straw and takes a sip. "Never thought I'd find Jacoby again."

15
OLIVIA, EIGHTY-EIGHT YEARS OLD (PRESENT TIME)

I'll be damned. That's him alright. My young, vital Jacoby has been hijacked and mangled. His Burt-Lancaster-style five o'clock shadow matured into a blanket of white stubble. His spine bends 90 degrees, causing the tip of his nose to lead his stride like he's stretching for the finish line. They say men age gracefully, but he's near ninety. His prime's waving at him in the rearview mirror.

We met when I was twenty-six and he was twenty-seven. We had nothing to lose and everything to gain, at least that's how we saw it. Distance and time simplify the complexity of a relationship. Like the oil in a salad dressing left to sit, the good memories separate from the bad, floating to the top when it needs to be shaken. Jacoby was many things, but after decades apart, he looks mighty saintly.

"Who is he?" June snakes her neck for a clear view.

I suck the juice box dry and crush it like a beer can. My strength's returned. "The love of my life," I answer.

"What?"

The brass bell rings. She doesn't have an opportunity for questions. He approaches the checkout counter, squinting and straining to read the menu's calligraphy. His crippled, arthritic finger points to the chalkboard. The barista notices and shoves his phone into his pocket, welcoming his order.

"What's that say?" Jacoby skips pleasantries. "How we suh-pose to read that? Is it English?"

"Ah yeah, bunch of squiggles, right? Lemme help." The barista scans the board to find the item in question. "You mean...croissant?"

"The hell it is." Jacoby slaps the counter, tacky from over-poured coffees. "Forget it. Just a bowl of water for my friend." The request is for Winston, whose wet nose presses the windowpane, licking his lips in anticipation. He'll soon be disappointed.

If it weren't for Jacoby's distinct, permanent scowl, I'd barely recognize him. It comes from forty years on a General Motors assembly line. His shirt was so filthy it'd drip grease, but the automotive grime never bothered him like the political filth dripping from the top tier. "That, you can't scrub clean," he'd say.

"Aunt Ol, what about Winston?" June whispers.

A muffled meow is heard through the glass. Winston's hungry.

"Shh!" I push her lips shut.

The barista returns with a ceramic ramekin filled with water. He offers it to Jacoby, who doesn't take it, but instead turns to walk. "This way, son." The boy takes the lead, a testament to his manners.

They close in on our table. I take a deep breath.

"Merry met, and merry part. I drink to thee with all my heart!" I yell.

Behind us, the white noise of conversation softens, lending way to the sultry voice of Smokey Robinson crooning through the speakers. June's fingernails dig into my thigh.

Jacoby halts abruptly. The barista, unprepared, rams into his crooked, protruding hip, splashing the water onto his own crotch. He maintains his composure. "No worries, I got it," he groans, skillfully hiding indignation, then crouches down to dry the spill.

Jacoby's not concerned. He takes a labored step closer, looking this old lady up and down. The chestnut hair he once knew diluted to a mousey, silver-streaked brown. The long lashes have fallen out, along with a few teeth. He's changed, but I have too. I pull a necklace from my bosom with a ring strung where a pendant would be; the design is two hands delicately holding a ruby in the shape of a heart. I lift it to catch the sunlight, and the gem sparkles as it oscillates.

His nose twitch makes his mustache shimmy. After another step his expression pales.

"Olivia, baby?" His cap covers his heart, exposing a cue-ball scalp. His lush hair managed to cling to his nape, but he couldn't save the top.

I flash a gummy smile. "You have my cat."

He looks to Winston. "The little fella's yours? As independent as his owner." He smiles, tripling the wrinkles on his pliant forehead.

A sharp pain, like repetitive bee stings, attacks my nerve endings. Low blood sugar was temporary relief from the third eye's burn, but with the nausea subsiding the throbbing returns and my senses enhance, the strongest being smell.

Retirement and countless showers have not diluted the scent of motor oil that has surely seeped into the base of his pores. But another, potent scent lingers, like an iron-scorched dress.

Anthony sniffs my blouse. "I hate to interrupt the lovefest, but do you smell something burning?"

The café lights flicker—once, twice, and then completely off—followed by a round of customer moans.

"What happened to the Wi-Fi?" A teenager emerges from the shield of his computer screen, white cords strung from his ears.

"Aunt Ol!" With a forceful blow, June extinguishes the flame dancing on the mitten. The eyeball eerily spins underneath the singed yarn, rolling like a marble. It's awake.

She grabs my arm. "We gotta get you out of here." The few strands left of the mitten unravel and fall.

"Wait a minute. What is *that*?!"

Her attempt is useless. Jacoby's found the palm's eye.

Anthony thinks fast. With a fistful of plaid he yanks him forward. "You're coming with us." Jacoby's resistant but out-muscled, shuffling to keep up. He swats at Anthony, catching air.

Sixty years ago he would've thrown a punch. He had a hell of a right hook and worked the underground fighting circuit. His Irish mother berated the barbaric hobby, but his father was prouder than all get-out.

"Who the hell do you think you are? *Don't you touch me*," he argues.

"Hey man, take it easy." The barista passively shows empty hands. He's innocently optimistic for a harmonious resolution.

A woman, middle-aged with a thick, curly mane, takes a confrontational approach, throwing a *Reader's Digest* that grazes Anthony's shoulder. "Hey, cut it out! Leave him be!"

A baby cries as his mother gasps. Jacoby's cursing, threatening legal action, while June escorts me by the straps of my bra.

Winston joins us outside, riled by the high-strung emotion. The van's parked across the street. Mystical waves of neon blues and greens seep from the cracked passenger window, forming a dusty fog over the hood.

"Jacoby, trust me on this," I plead. Sparks spit from my fingertips. "I'll explain in a minute, but you must come, whether you like it or not."

A solid kick to Anthony's shin frees him. He stops at the curb, zeroed in on the necklace. "Which way does the heart face?"

He'd explained the rules when he gifted his ma's Claddagh ring: "Wear the ring on the right hand with the point of the heart toward your fingertips, and you's single and looking for love. If the point of the heart is toward your wrist, then you's taken. Now, if you wear the ring on your left hand with the point of the heart toward the fingertips, you's engaged. On the left hand with the point toward the wrist, well, you's married." Arthritis has swelled my knuckles, forcing me to wear it as a necklace, but I still made sure of one detail.

"Since the day you entered my life, the heart has *always* pointed toward my wrist."

A smile splits his bristled jaw.

"Come on, old man." Brashly, Anthony sweeps Jacoby from the ground like a bride about to go over a threshold, acutely aware of café patrons devising intervention. June has Winston in a headlock, a much lighter load, and arrives at the van first. She thrusts open its sliding door for a quick entry, tossing Winston in first, who lands with the finesse of a hippopotamus. All the time, the third eye rapidly wiggles, surveying the area and seeking its jeweled cohort.

June finds the box hidden under her seat. The cool lights reflect on her sweaty, glistening skin. Anthony starts the engine and speeds off, running the first stop sign he encounters. In the distance is the exodus of the café as they line the sidewalk, baffled by the anarchic escape.

"Aunt Ol, look!" June waves a tri-fold piece of paper over the headrest. "A delivery."

It comes from the box, but unlike those that came before, I recognize this offering. In fact, at one time, I demanded it was made. I've lost track of it over the years, maybe intentionally, I don't know. I needed to move on. Now the document's returned, but it's not meant for me, at least not me alone.

"Give it to him." I motion to Jacoby.

Cautiously, he unfolds the delicate paper. Dark, thick ink letters scrawl across the top margin and layer an embossed, raised government seal. The letters read: "Certificate of Birth."

"Our baby." His eyes glisten with unshed tears.

"Olivi-aaaa." June quivers. The jewelry box is convulsing, irritated at being confined within her crossed arms. It pops free, smacking the van's ceiling and, like a winding-down dreidel, settles atop Jacoby's velcro sneakers. The iris of the palm's eye transforms to match the hypnotic hues of the opals. *It's happening*.

"Anthony, we need you to stay here. Keep driving, I don't care where to." I force my fingers to link with June's, zapping her with a bolt of electricity. She squirms for freedom, so I tighten my grip.

"You're coming with us," I order. "When we're gone, no one will be left to carry on her memory."

Wasting no more time, I pinch the top of the paper while Jacoby holds the bottom. The jewelry box's blinding light returns, fracturing into thirds and taking three souls to another realm.

16

JACOBY, TWENTY-NINE YEARS OLD (SIXTY YEARS AGO)

"Breathe, baby, breathe." I can't lose her, too.

The nurse was alarmed when she discovered we weren't married. "I see," she said, judging me, the only man left in the waiting room, while the other, married fathers went to smoke.

A crinkled cloth separates the obstetric team from Olivia and I, or at least from Olivia's head. The rest of her body is stripped bare, veiled to maintain her modesty and to protect me from the gruesome visual. But it's pointless. Doctors come and go while Olivia's spread legs display mutilated genitals, her feet strapped into two metal stirrups hinged to bedposts.

She's been given scopolamine and morphine, a drug combination used to induce twilight sleep. "She's heavily sedated," Dr. Schultz assures. "She won't feel a thing."

His words are shallow. The sight of Olivia in such a state makes me ill. She thrashes her arms, provoking and swatting nurses like bothersome flies. Blood and feces smear the hospital bed, and though I was given fair warning, the comparisons to a pig after slaughter are undeniable as her cervix stretches to create an opening for our child.

"Sally."

"Yes, doctor."

"I'm going to transfer the infant to you."

The nurse readies her position, holding the white cloth like she's anticipating the snap of a football. Focus over chaos, knowledge over naivety. The curtain separates degrees of competency. Olivia and I are helpless. So is our baby.

"I fear she's asphyxiated. Is the isolette ready?"

"Yes, doctor."

There are six others in the room. Five wear pale green gowns, the shade opposite red on the color wheel. Makes it easier to spot blood.

My knowledge of medical jargon is pathetic. Damn my education, or lack thereof. My hands are qualified for car parts, not delicate surgeries. I don't belong here. Breech birth, asphyxia, risk of hemorrhage, arterial thrombosis, it's as if they're conversing in Gaelic, gargling when they speak.

"Can you see anything?" Olivia is delirious, twitching and spouting incoherent sounds. The nurse brought leather shackles but Olivia's just tame enough to stay unchained. I rubberneck around the powder-blue curtain to gather evidence for a report.

"He's about to take 'em out," I whisper. Olivia seems pleased, but reacts by nibbling her tongue.

Not a second later, Dr. Schultz holds our baby high, nearly brushing the bulb that lies above the bed with mucus-drenched hair. The bright lighting enhances what I was afraid of. Through a film of red blood, our baby's face is a deep blue. No screaming. No signs of life.

Dr. Schultz begins suctioning the nose and throat with what looks like a turkey baster. Still nothing.

"Sally, apply the bag-valve mask while I stabilize the child. We have to puff her."

I clasp Olivia's hand, but my eyes are on our baby. "Her," *the doctor* told Sally. *We have a girl.* But Dr. Schultz doesn't introduce us. He's preoccupied. Focused.

A contraption is positioned over the baby's nose and mouth that resembles a Soviet gas mask, and in quick, forceful squeezes a balloon thrusts air into her lungs. It's a dizzying scene. A second doctor approaches and washes his hands at the sink, preparing to assist. Dr. Schultz notices and provides instruction. "Dr. Donnell, I trust that you'll monitor the mother." Dutifully, he goes to Olivia. "Her last injection was at half past noon," Dr. Schultz explains. "The effects may wear off shortly."

"She's not crying!" Olivia bellows. Dr. Donnell clears his throat as a cue for me to get my woman under control, then leaves for the tray where the shackles are waiting. Olivia bites her lip, eyes wide, desperate for answers. "Jacoby, why isn't she crying?" Furiously, she shakes her head and slings the cotton-wool earplugs Sally had inserted to dampen noise.

But I don't respond, because I don't know. The youngest nurse approaches, a student by the looks of the square, napkin-like hat plopped atop her blond bouffant. "Congratulations. You, ah, you have a baby girl." Her forced, nervous smile wants to say it'll be OK, but her stutter relays uncertainty.

Over her shoulder, the rest of the team huddles around our baby. A clear, rectangular box with two circular openings stands to the left of them. Inside is a small bed waiting to be filled.

"What's wrong with her?" Olivia demands. The young nurse winces, wiping her hands repeatedly on her stark white skirt. She looks to Sally for help, but gets nothing. She's twenty at most, an amateur at unexpected misfortune. She flaunts her inexperience. "Ah, ah..."

Dr. Schultz catches the nurse making matters worse, while Dr. Donnell eyes the measurements on a filling syringe, preparing to administer another dose. "Sally, go get her," he orders, then turns his back toward our table, completely blocking our view. "I can't have this, her causing trouble. Please...tend to the parents. They'll need your comfort soon."

Soon? What's happening *soon*? With his concentration broken, his quick-paced motions slow, then stop. A deep exhale. He steps away from the incubator where our baby lies and bows his head, moving his lips without discernible sound. Hands clasped. He's praying.

He begins wiping the blood from the baby's skin with a white muslin cloth, going carefully around the tubes strung from her tiny arms and throat.

Sally grabs the young nurse by the shoulders. "Have a seat, Joyce."

Joyce, noticeably upset, nods and walks backward toward the room's entrance, ashamed of her mumbling and inability to work under pressure. She brushes a tear from her cheek.

"As Joyce said, you have a baby girl," Sally begins.

"What's *wrong* with her? Why can't we see her?"

"Miss, you need to calm down. You've lost a lot of bl—"

"No! I want my child. *Please.*" Olivia shakes from her collarbone to the top of her scalp, eyes squinted, mouth clenched with teeth exposed. I kiss her hairline. She's exhausted. She's endured a marathon labor. From my understanding, throughout the twenty-four-hour ordeal, nothing went as planned but it was at least under control.That is, until the situation turned for the worse and I was brought in.

Olivia breaks, releasing a flood of anguish.

"Ma'am, please..." Dr. Donnell steps in. With a swift punch, the tip of the syringe stabs Olivia's flesh. On the table is a cloth soaked in chloroform, reinforcements in case the medication's effects are delayed.

"Breathe, baby," I whisper, tenderly brushing her hair. Despite this, or because of this, she's beautiful. A warrior whose body faced a crucible, withstanding what I'd thought was physically impossible.

Dr. Schultz steps forward. He's in his early forties, a young doctor compared to his peers. He removes his gloves, then squares his stance, bare hands clasped over his pelvis. "Dad, come with me."

Through drooping eyes, Olivia shoots me a look that could cut through granite. I delay, hesitant to leave her, but Sally takes over smoothing her hair. "We'll explain in a minute, miss," she soothes. "There were complications, but now we need you to relax." Olivia caves, only partially aware of her surroundings, but aware enough to know that she has no choice.

"She's beautiful. I'm so sorry..." He stops himself. There's a quiver in his voice. Discreetly, he sniffles and twitches his nose while faking an itchy septum.

"Is she..."

"Not yet. She's alive, but it's hard to estimate for how long. She went too long without oxygen in the womb. A blood clot traveled through the umbilical cord during labor and blocked her supply. We could rush her to the NICU, perhaps grant her another hour, if that, or maybe longer. It's difficult to tell. We resuscitated her, but she's unable to breathe on her own. She had no response to our stimulation tests. At this point, I've done all I can."

I look back at Olivia, who has fallen asleep, succumbed to the wooziness of the drugs and sleep deprivation. Sally dabs her forehead with a washcloth.

The slow beating of a tiny heart is the only difference between a real baby and a doll. She couldn't wait until her due date. Born two months early, her body is slightly larger than my fist. I wish I could say she resembles Olivia, but I'd be lying. Her minuscule features are too petite to resemble anyone. Still, from the outside she is a perfectly proportionate human—ten fingers, ten toes. She doesn't have the fat rolls I remember layering my siblings, like a stack of hot dogs without the buns. Her insides paint another picture, with lungs half-formed and a brain pleading for the nutrients needed to develop.

I hear whispers in the background.

"She'll be a vegetable."

"Her APGAR score's the lowest I've seen."

"Muscle tone was zero."

"Do we rush her to the NICU?"

"No, there's no use, she's got minutes, if that."

"Let's go, our job here is done."

How can I reverse this? Can I pray harder, close my eyes and pretend it's not happening, make them all go away? I'm tempted to shake Olivia. Wake her and demand she give the final say: to give our baby more time, or let her go. Olivia knows her better. She carried her, nourished her, protected her. Aside from giving my sperm, I've done nothing for this child.

The time between beats lengthens. The skin covering her chest is no thicker than a piece of tracing paper. *Ba-bump, ba-bump.* I reach in through the case's hole and touch her hand to introduce myself. I use my thumb and index finger to shake her tiny palm like a business meeting introduction.

"Nice to meet you, baby girl." My chest pinches my heart, slowing its beats to sync with hers. It's then that the hard truth sets in. This moment is irreversible. No do-over labor. Our baby is teetering between realms and there's not a damn thing anyone can do to make her stay.

And suddenly, pushing through the grief is another emotion. Anger.

Anger for the loss of a family that will never come to be, for missing Olivia's voice singing her to sleep, and for having to inform our family and friends that the perfect, uncomplicated pregnancy ended in unforeseen tragedy. Their sympathy will come but I wish it wouldn't. They can keep their funeral casseroles, and their awkward silences, and their fumbled, rambling condolences. Desperately, I pray for the laws of nature to show leniency, for death to be reasonable and find a different, matured companion to befriend today.

Dr. Schultz has not moved, nor has Sally, who is patiently stationed near Olivia. They are solemnly aware of what I'm just discovering. Soon I will not have a choice in our baby's care. Her heart is beating on borrowed time.

"I have a theory," his authoritative voice tempers. His shoulder is next to mine. The relationship of doctor to patient has dissolved. We are standing man to man.

"I've been doing this for over a decade, delivering babies, and I'd be hard-pressed to find anyone who fights harder for their life than an infant. The tenacity of wanting to live starts before we can perceive why we'd want to bother trying. It's innate."

As he speaks, I trace the veins of her foot, visible through sheer, unhardened skin.

"Through it all, I've come to believe this. That the concept of time is meaningless when it comes to love. We do not value love by how long we receive it, but instead by how powerful it was during the time we were given to share it. It's the best way I can rationalize a life taken unjustly. Your daughter, her time may feel short, but the amount of love she's experiencing is immense."

With a jolt, my stomach wedges into my throat. "Rhona," I whisper.

"Pardon?"

"Our daughter. She was meant to be a Rhona. It's Irish. It means powerful. Mighty."

His glances over with a soft, condolatory smile. "It's fitting."

"May I?"

He nods.

I lift Rhona's head into the palm of my hand and her neck goes limp. I want her out of the plastic case. I want to hold my warm child, not her corpse.

Dr. Schultz helps maneuver the tubes and carefully lowers Rhona into the hammock my arms create. He gathers the cords like a tangled vacuum's while I move at a tightrope walker's pace, one foot in front of the other, toward Olivia.

Sally offers her chair when I arrive. Though languishing, Olivia's eyelids refuse to close, exposing only the whites as her pupils roll back. I draw the blanket from Rhona's chest. Limply, her arm flops free, then she sucks in a struggling breath.

"My baby." Olivia wakes. She caresses Rhona's face, a touch so gentle it doesn't leave an indent. "She's...what she was meant to be. She's perfection."

"Of course she is." I inch closer. "She's half you."

Olivia taps Rhona's teeny fingertips, equal attention placed on each. "I'm a mom."

"I, ah, named her Rhona."

Her expression lightens.

"I love it."

I was hoping she would.

I'm skirting around the news, afraid the morphine will hinder her comprehension and mottle the seriousness of Rhona's prognosis.

"I don't wanna say goodbye," Olivia whispers. It's a matter-of-fact statement without an overdramatic delivery. Whether she overheard the conversations or it's intuition, somehow, she knows.

Rhona shivers as her warmth fades. Her cheeks are pink and swollen. Her feathery lashes stick straight out from slit eyelids. Her feet, the size of gumballs, snuggle into the cotton hospital blanket and puzzle-piece themselves into the inner crease of my elbow.

Sally watches from across the room. She's the only one left. The minutes have gathered, the surgical utensils are cleaned, the doctors have moved on to the next patient, the next life.

"Wrap her arms, she's chilled." Olivia draws circles on Rhona's tiny bicep, then transitions to a sweeping line up and down her slender arm, feeling for a pulse below her armpit before allowing the swaddle. Then, Olivia says what I fear: "She let go."

Sally steps in and confirms the finding. "Do you want a moment?"

Olivia requests to hold her. Though at first hesitant, knowing the medication torrents her system, Sally agrees. She places Rhona atop her mother's bosom, and with a tender, glissando voice, Olivia sings:

"A-a-a, a-a-a,
były sobie kotki dwa.
A-a-a, kotki dwa,
szarobure, szarobure obydwa.
Ach, śpij, kochanie,
jesli gwiazdke z nieba chcesz—dostaniesz.
Wszystkie dzieci, nawet źle,
pogrążone są we śnie,
a ty jedna tylko nie."

"Kotki dwa"—two cats. A Polish lullaby, likely a favorite of her mother or father.

Gently, I kiss her forehead, then her cheek, and as I pull away, I interlock my fingers with hers. As I do, the surgical light above our head flickers, creating a stop-motion effect. With each flash, I pick a new spot on her face to admire, and when I get to her eyes, I feel my soul yanked from my chest, gone from this moment.

17
ANTHONY, TWENTY-EIGHT YEARS OLD (PRESENT TIME)

I'm driving aimlessly with a gas tank near empty, passing street after street of blighted, rundown homes waiting for a bulldozer, empty lots with grass growing as tall as my knees and little hope of a manicure.

It's fitting, really. Just like the three bodies sprawled out in my van, these homes have lost their souls.

Olivia and Jacoby are like wax figures curated by Madame Tussauds, except their wrinkles give the impression of neglect by the sculptor, as if they were left to rot in the sun. Olivia's decent looking, fully alive, but when a physical body is void of a soul it's virtually unrecognizable. Attend any funeral with an open casket and this is apparent. There they are, skin slathered with makeup like a newscaster about to go live on air. Their loved ones scratch their heads, "Did Nana wear eyeliner?" Let down by the disconnect of what they see to the semblance they're desperate to keep close. Without a soul the flame's been snuffed, even in the most authentically preserved corpse. I have a preview of her funeral's main attraction.

Then there's June, sunk into the seat, limbs flopped and distorted. She's vulnerable, dead weight. Her long, bony fingers extend from floppy wrists that attach to beanpole arms. She still wears her wedding ring, now way too loose.

"Now where?" I'm talking to Winston, a cat. He's rolled into a ball on the dashboard. He shows no interest in conversation.

I turn up the radio for company. *Welcome back to WOMC 104.3, Detroit's Greatest Hits. Up next the vocal styling of Freddie Mercury and the British rock band Queen, with their 1980 hit, "Another One Bites the Dust."*

The catchy baseline kicks in, with its steady beat bringing flashbacks of chest compressions on a CPR dummy. A class I failed—twice—and ruined my high school career as a summer lifeguard at Veterans Memorial Park. Soon, my lip curls and shoulders strut, lost in the vibrato of Freddie Mercury's vocals, until verse two, when the faint, tri-tone alert of a text message interrupts the melody.

It's June's cell phone.

I scan the floorboard with one hand on the wheel. It's likely Linda, freaking out. She expected June to be home after her hospital shift. If June's reply time to a message exceeds fifteen minutes, Linda always calls. She worries about June, even more so lately. She'd stop at nothing to ensure June's safety, and given all the loved ones she's lost and recently taken in, I can't help but feel for the woman.

I shuffle through a mess of unpaid parking tickets. "Where'd she put it?" The box is nestled near Jacoby's feet. The opals are commanding, directing beams of light to Olivia's hand. It's weirdly quiet. Freakishly quiet.

The phone beeps again. The screen lights up the cubby on the passenger side door, where June stashed it for safekeeping, along with the pager from our guide.

The last time she travelled, I barely touched her and seared my finger. If I try for the phone and make contact, I'll either get sucked in or blown up. "Fuck!" I almost clear her legs when the case slips.

The phone plummets, stick-straight like a pencil dive, then ricochets off June's knee, and on its way down, clips the pager. The force of the blow catapults the pager, sending it soaring above her lap. A split-second later it lands on June's crotch, wedged between the crack of her thighs, deep in the crevice of her jeans, encased by her body's heat. Black smoke seeps from the device, but June stays still. The pager's overheating and about to combust.

In a hysterical, impulsive fog, I rip off my shirt for an insulator, kick open the door, and shot-put the pager into the road. It explodes mid-air with a gunshot bang.

"Anthony!" June shrieks. "What the hell are you doing? *Why is your shirt off?*" She grabs the armrest for support, still woozy from the trip. I'm bare-chested, one foot lodged in a pothole, uncomfortably exposed.

She pieces together what happened. "Now what are we supposed to do?" she cries. Clasped fingers support her skull while she helplessly looks to the sky. June kicks the largest chunk left of the ravaged plastic into the curb. Winston joins her, sniffing the remains. Broken bits scatter like confetti.

The realization hits. I have destroyed the only source of communication with the lone person who has *any* clue of what we've gotten ourselves into.

18

JUNE, TWENTY-EIGHT YEARS OLD (PRESENT TIME)

I'm livid, standing amidst the pager's rubble. "Why can't you control yourself?" The irony makes me laugh. "But of course, what did I expect? If you can't keep your pants zipped, you surely can't wait five minutes to answer a text message."

"I was trying to do you a favor! I thought it was Linda," he argues. His intentions may have been good, but what he in fact did was destroy our only lifeline for a message reminding me that my birth control prescription was filled at CVS.

"You did it again, Anth. You did it again."

That was the fifth trip, after which clear instructions were given to page Meira, but now we're shit out of luck.

On top of that, Olivia and Jacoby just returned from a trip of heartache only they can comprehend, and Anthony can't grant them the time to process the experience before creating mayhem. Accident or not, his reckless core thrives on being the center of attention, showing no mercy to innocent bystanders.

He spins, hands on his hips. "I fucked up, alright? Pardon me for trying to be considerate to *your* mom."

I could tackle him right here. Right now. I count my breaths; I find a focus point on the ground, anything to keep from exploding.

He's putting the blame on me. Classic. I didn't show affection, so he cheated. I stopped putting out, so he got it elsewhere. I got the job, had loving parents, a solid group of friends, all the components to a blessed life, so I got what I deserved: a failed marriage. It *couldn't* be his fault. The universe decided I was due for a little suffering.

I always chalked up this dark side of Anthony to genetics, to a childhood of continual blows. There'll always be something, or someone, to point his finger at.

"Why'd you come this morning, Anthony? Before you knew all this would happen. Don't say because of the jewelry box. You and I both know that's bullshit. You could have left it and ran."

"Let's not get into this."

"And why not?" I can feel my courage building. "Was your life dull again? You needed a little chaos to spice it up, so you thought you'd return to where you got your last fix? You got rid of coke and booze, so I guess inflating your ego at my expense is the next best thing."

I bite my lip, collecting my thoughts. The opportunity has come and I want to get this right. I want him to feel my pain, but I realize empathy passed over him at birth. "Do you care about how this affects me? Tell me this: what do you value? That's what I want to know, because I learned a *long time* ago that it wasn't your wife or the vows said before two hundred of our closest friends and family."

"Maybe I don't *value* anything!" he blurts.

The honesty is refreshing, a swig of cold water for this parched enabler.

While he sat on his air-conditioned throne, falling deeply in love with his reflection, I swatted criticisms of him, of our relationship, with kung-fu reflexes—from friends, family, even strangers overhearing degrading remarks while we waited for the check on our anniversary dinner. "It's not my place, but he shouldn't speak to you like that." "Don't let him boss you." A quick bathroom trip to wipe mascara-stained cheeks turned into a counseling session by silver-haired, one-time debutantes drenched in Joan Rivers's perfume.

"You know why we worked for so many years?" he continues, keen to my brewing resentment.

"Because I sadistically revel in the fact that your nonsense makes me out to be an angel in comparison?"

"Wow. Was that a slip of the tongue?" His retort is quick, and I'm not prepared to answer. I shrug and turn my cheek, embarrassed. I've never admitted it out loud, or at all, but I think...I meant it.

Anthony punches the van, but half-assed. He's learned to calm his temper. Stepping back, he tugs his pants up and above his overhanging belly, then leans against the hood. His supportive forearm is on display, the same forearm used to lift the secretary onto a table in the break room and screw her until a new tenant barged in. The kid only wanted a slice of free, welcome-to-your-new-home pizza, but struck gold with hardcore porn instead.

Jacoby and Olivia cautiously creep to their seat's edge, prepared to step in if needed.

"No, *I'll* tell you why," he concludes, his pitch lowered. "It's because you're the only one willing—or dumb enough—to put up with me. Any other person would have kicked me to the curb, but you left the door open for me to return. You were the perfect child who never made a wrong choice, and it made you jealous that I could leave, live recklessly, take chances, and then return when I pleased and pick up where I left off. But *you* allowed it. You waited for me, welcomed me with open arms."

He's convinced he has me pegged. He's ripped the veil from our relationship, shed light onto subconscious actions that fueled the strength of our bond—our dependency.

"You know *nothing* about how I've survived without you," I counter.

"You can't be serious? June, I know you better than you know yourself." The familiar degrading tone questions my intelligence, raised eyebrows and crinkled forehead screaming *duh!*

Not this time.

"*You're wrong*," I blast. My posture stiffens. "You're the prodigal son, eh? I'll confess, you are true to the character. Once again, the story revolves around egotistical, everybody-loves-me, always-get-my-way *you*. In fact, the whole fucking world revolves around you."

He's silent.

The words from the parable flash before my eyes like the scrolling digital screens of Times Square. I can see the Bible's page, corners covered with handwritten notes for direction, like *SPEAK LOUDLY* and *SMILE*. At ten years old, I was the narrator in our Sunday-school performance. Every holiday the tape somehow replays.

My son, the father said, you are always with me, and everything I have is yours. But we had to celebrate and be glad, because this brother of yours was dead and is alive again; he was lost and is found.

I pause, internalizing the words like never before.

"You know what? The lost son isn't the pillar of the parable, nor is the good son who stayed. The *father* is. Maybe, like good ol' Dad, we are referees to two sides of ourselves. One is a bit crazy and the other is sane. It's unavoidable that at some point we'll lose our minds, but if we keep hoping and learn to embrace our fucked-up, crazy side, we can finally make peace with our flaws and be whole again."

Anthony just stands there. I can't stop. Pent-up anger has been unleashed.

"For years, I was a lunatic, convincing myself it was healthy to have you in my life. I never had to run off and be reckless. I stayed home and was reckless. *You* are my reckless, but trying to sweep my own crazy under the rug prevents me from moving on. It's a part of me, and I must accept that. I need to realize I'm lost, put in the work, and make amends."

"June." Finally, he stops my rant but says no more. I've hijacked his attempt to twist history.

We're drained. All of us. Jacoby rubs his eyes, swallowing spit to suppress nausea. Olivia's a pitbull, ready to attack for my honor but chained to her seat by decrepit, worn joints. Even Anthony now squats on the curb, at a loss for what to do or say.

I find the afternoon sun and stare straight into the blazing center. I feel the tissue of my retinas weaken, knowing I'd be defenseless if the sun should choose to flex its solar muscle. The circle takes shape as my vision adjusts to its intensity, the eye in the sky watching our every move, its rays consuming all that falls in its path.

"How about you take me home?" Jacoby hollers, cleaning smudges on his spectacles with a linen handkerchief, a pocket staple for men of his generation.

Through the tension we all crack smiles. It's needed comedic relief. We've exhausted words, now all we can do is make our next move.

"Might as well," I conclude. I gather the broken remains of the pager and scoop Winston into my arms. Anthony grabs an extra shirt from the trunk, a size too small. He hasn't updated his emergency kit.

Inside, Jacoby clasps the top of Olivia's hand. The swelling has subsided. The eye's lid has closed tight and the color tamed back to pale from hot pink. The elixir was Jacoby, at least this time. He finally breaks the hold when Anthony revs the engine, caressing the ridges and folds of her malleable skin with each fingertip as he pulls away.

"Head to the corner of St. Aubin and East Warren, and I'll take it from there," he directs. He breaks into a coughing fit that has me concerned he'll pop a lung. "Just a tickle in my throat," he shrugs off, but the tickle doesn't resolve. He beats his chest, trying to dislodge stubborn phlegm. The handkerchief covers his mouth to muffle the noise. He's quick to shove the cloth into his pocket, but not quick enough to hide the specks of blood. It strikes me that his cheeks are sunken but his gut is rotund. The beard covers it well. His body has chosen the areas it wants to eat away.

Still, he appears content, almost peaceful. The jewelry box gave Jacoby what he needed, and looking at Olivia's expression, the solace she was seeking as well. But unlike Jacoby's, there's complexity in her smile. Without a way to reach our guide, she is bound to be the sacrificial lamb in this grand adventure, destined to suffer for the benefit of the group.

The pager's scorched plastic shell rests in the cup holder. I bow my head and say a silent prayer, not to God. No, not this time, at least not the detached, esoteric God I once imagined. I pray to the silence, requesting a little assistance with the mess we've found ourselves in.

19

OLIVIA, EIGHTY-EIGHT YEARS OLD (PRESENT TIME)

Anthony slows to a snail's pace. "No, no, not yet," Jacoby corrects. "At the next block, take a right."

He narrows the space between our bucket seats. His arched back brings his mouth close with little effort, aiding his wanted secrecy. "Will you be OK?" he whispers. Playfully, I push him away. He swivels at the hip like a hinged door.

"Of course. Don't worry about me."

This last trip, through Jacoby, my soul gained a lucid perspective. The outcome was unchanged, but I can recall the beauty in every detail. Her rose-tinted cheeks, a nose no bigger than my pinky nail. I remember her. My Rhona. My father's death may have opened my eyes, but she fueled the need for understanding, for peace.

"I can take care of myself."

Jacoby smiles. "That you can."

Truthfully, I'm not as confident as my forced assurance, but having Jacoby worry won't help the situation. If anything, keeping him around will make the journey more complicated. I'm no spring chicken, but two ailing elders would make the ratio of able-bodies to physical-liabilities fifty-fifty.

We drive along train tracks. Clouds take over the sky, masking the sun and forming an upside-down sea of gray water vapor. The severity of the blight strikes me.

My hope for Detroit lies in souls like Jacoby. The people hiding behind the walls of the century-old brick homes only to come out on Sundays and immerse themselves in the community, to mingle with the moms and pops running cafés and supermarkets, to hold on to the businesses fending off bankruptcy.

"Here we are. Park tight to the curb, will ya." We've arrived at an apartment complex near Eastern Market. Jacoby unbuckles his seat belt, preparing to exit.

"You live *here*? We're four miles from the café! How'd you get there?" Anthony asks in disbelief.

"Walked," he answers matter-of-factly. "The exercise is good for me."

"No wonder you made it to ninety."

Anthony turns off the engine and walks around the vehicle to help Jacoby. June slides open the door on my side. "Wanna say goodbye?"

"What? You want me to kiss him goodnight?"

June laughs. "Only if you want to. It's the twenty-first century, feminism is a thing now."

"It's always been a thing in the right circles." I wink.

Jacoby clasps my elbow for balance, but it's also an expression of tenderness. We walk two-by-two toward his apartment complex, a historic Beaux-Arts red brick building framed with limestone quoins, evidence of Detroit's connection to France. Elegant steel balustrades lead to a towering door made for a regal giant. At one time, the complex was home to the king of the city's crop, and in my opinion, it still is.

We reach the entrance. Anthony and June keep their distance, giving us privacy.

"Jacoby, my love." I haven't said that since I was in my twenties. His stubbly white cheeks turn rosy pink.

"Olivia, my doll." He kisses the top of my hand. "I never lost admiration for you."

"For *me*? I was the one who left."

"We grew apart," he interjects, reluctant to hear my self-deprecation, but I can't let him be the martyr. I may not get the chance to say this again.

"I was jealous of you, do you know that?" I admit. He squints, confused. His overgrown brows eclipse his eyes.

I continue. "You accepted what happened, always so calm. In the weeks to follow, you never questioned that there was something to be gained from Rhona's death, whereas I was spitting fire at a universe that stripped away what was ours. It took me a while to get to that place. I couldn't expect you to wait for me."

"I would have," he blurts. A risky statement, but he's in good hands now. We're too old for games. He has nothing to lose. "Even when you walked out that door for the final time, I couldn't be mad at you. You know what I did? I walked to the window and watched you drive away, and I said, 'Thank you.' I said it out loud, to no one, and I meant it. I was in a place in my life where I knew I could go on without you, so I wished you well. You needed to go."

They are the sweetest words ever said to me. Sweeter than I love you, which keeps the speaker as the focus—*I* love you. Thank *you* is selfless and shows gratitude for the acts and efforts of another. Squeezing his hand, I return the sentiment. "*Thank you*."

I fish down my shirt for Rhona's birth certificate, trapped between my armpit fat and elastic bra strap. Smiling, he accepts the gift and stashes it in the front pocket of his button-down shirt.

"Good day, Olivia." He opens the door, but pauses after placing one foot inside. He points to Anthony. "Hey, young man."

Anthony cautiously steps forward. "Yeah?"

"I don't know what demons you're fighting," Jacoby begins.

"Sir, I'm not—"

Jacoby holds his hand up, ceasing interruptions. "You can listen or not. Frankly, I don't care. But, I overheard that argument."

Anthony is silent, submissive, his chin down.

Theatrically clearing his throat, Jacoby continues. "My belief is that there's a power, a sacredness in this world that deserves respect. That has *value* greater than the individual. I could give a flying rat's ass what you address that power *as*, if you give it a name at all. I have my opinions, but I can't guarantee they are right."

Anthony straightens his posture to look up, now listening.

Jacoby returns his gaze. "Perhaps that power is toying with us, hidden within—not separate from—the science and math we study. Perhaps we can't grasp it because we don't understand it, at least not yet. That is my hunch. If that power is personal or not, if it hears your every prayer or you've been speaking to deaf ears, well, that's up to you to decide, but I beg of you: don't lose hope. Keep searching. Find the sacredness in the faces that surround you, even if it takes you four miles one-way to reach a place where you finally can appreciate it. We're like pennies, ya know? Just one is worth almost nothing, but collect them and little by little they'll add up."

Anthony mildly nods, a slight smile forming. "Yes, sir."

Jacoby tilts his hat and leaves for his apartment. His warm eyes find mine and maintain contact until the door slams shut.

Winston jumps onto the porch and scratches at the glass. "Sorry, Winnie. Our friend is gone."

A feral, grayish-brown cat joins him, lurking from under the deteriorating concrete porch, its humble home. Its fur is matted and caked with dried dirt.

"Shoo!" It scampers under the shrubbery, taking the hint it's not welcome. I pick up Winnie, my spine bending backward from his heft.

"I got him." June comes to my aid while Anthony offers me his elbow for balance.

Almost to the van, I pause, wondering if I'll revisit this moment one day. My peripheral vision catches a tiny head playing peek-a-boo behind a tree trunk, the feral cat hiding.

"*Kotki dwa.*" I smile. The irony is not lost on me. On the second story of the building, an arm pulls a heavy, swagged maroon curtain across the window. "*Śpij, kochanie.*"

20

ANTHONY, TWENTY-EIGHT YEARS OLD (PRESENT TIME)

We're back in the van and no one acknowledges the obvious. We have *no fucking clue* what to do next.

Olivia's sober reflection monopolizes my rearview mirror. "You good?" I ask.

She examines her palm, afraid to jinx the peace with a premature response. The eye's suspiciously tranquil—no swelling, no glowing. "I'm good," she decides. "For now." She's reserved, still coming down from the high of Jacoby's goodbye.

June is flipping the busted pager onto its side, utilizing the window's natural light for a better inspection. Aggravated, she hurls it at the glovebox. The jagged, broken plastic rips the van's upholstered leather. I bite my lip. I'm in the doghouse. Now's not the time to request she respect my belongings.

A crinkled, ketchup-stained napkin fans out of the cup holder. I pluck it out, wipe the excess sauce onto my pants, and hand it to June with a pen. "Alright, come on. Were there *any* useable clues from Lenny? Did he hint where this woman lived?" My forced optimism is pathetic, but it's better than guilt.

June's reluctant, but accepts. "Nope. Just that her name was Meira. We don't even have a last name to Google."

"I remember something," Olivia offers, sarcastically enthused. "He said I'd be in a crap-load of pain."

It wasn't the start I wanted, but she's bracing for the worst, and I can't blame her. Whether it's leaving Jacoby, nearly passing out, or Lenny's unpleasant premonition, the day is wearing on her.

"Yep, I remember that part, too." June throws me a deadpan stare. She crumples the napkin and reclines the backrest, swatting the torn, drooping fabric of the interior liner. She covers her eyes, defeated. Once again, I let her down.

"What else?" I urge. I'm pulling teeth from a lady who has none. "There has to be *something*."

I watch Olivia in the rearview mirror. She finds a loose cigarette in her purse and lights up. "Roll your window down, will ya?"

I oblige.

Perfect smoke circles travel through the open air. Her long fingers reach between my seat and the van's frame, dusting the ash on the window ledge. After a few long puffs, she's calmer.

"I get what you're trying to do—be the hero—but don't. The damage is done. *Move on*." She takes another steady, smooth drag. "The answer's obvious, because it's the only one. We need to continue to where my 'soul was stirred.' We need to keep going toward my childhood home. If this lady doesn't hear from us, it'd make sense that she meets us there, right? If she's so seasoned at soul-chasing, she should know these things. After all, she found *your* house." The lit end of the stick points at June.

It's a common-sense rationale, and honestly, we have no other option. I just hope Olivia's prepared for the worst if there's a delay, or our guide doesn't come at all. Our only saving grace is the olivewood coaster. At least that'll buy Olivia time.

June raps her fingertips on her forehead and finally concludes, "It's better than sitting here."

Olivia shrugs and taps off ash, this time onto the floor mat. "We'll see."

I shove the key into the ignition. The battery putters and nudges while I hold my breath. I take the momentum and shift the gear into drive. We approach the four-way stop as a repetitive, dinging noise activates.

"Shit." My brow pounds the wheel, sounding the horn. The miniature gas pump begins to blink green. "We're on E." Once again, my tail's between my legs.

The van decelerates, though I haven't eased off the gas pedal. "Fuckin' A. Can't catch a break."

Olivia snickers behind me. "*Now*, we've hit rock bottom."

About a mile away, eight city blocks, sits a Shell station. We run on fumes and roll toward the closest free pump.

A convenience store is connected to the station, reminding me that all I've eaten today is coffee and Olivia's recycled nicotine.

"I'm gonna run in. Want anything?"

"Nah." June's cleaning dirt from her nails, a nervous habit. "Wait." She cracks the door. "Changed my mind. I could use a bathroom." She turns to Olivia. "What about you, Aunt Ol?"

Olivia finishes her cigarette, and then, with dart-like precision, propels the torched nub through the open window. "Maybe another pack of Marlboros, and a Little Debbie cake. It'll be my last meal."

"Stop that," June snaps, then softly, "Any particular kind?"

"Surprise me."

The store's artificial lighting is depressing. The air conditioning is roaring, overcompensating for the heat outside. I never understood that logic. We wait all year for summer in Michigan. What's wrong with opening a window?

The clerk hands June the key for the restroom. "First door on the left, doll. Past the ATM."

I peruse the aisles, contemplating if I should risk food poisoning with cheddar-filled sausages spinning on the warming rack or stick with a pre-packaged, safer bet.

I toss a bag of Chex Mix and a Pepsi on the counter. There's a sale on Tic Tacs. "And these." I add them to my tower of processed sugar.

"Six seventy-five." The clerk avoids eye contact, punching the code to open the cashier drawer, impatiently waiting. I'd guess he's mid-sixties, overdue for retirement. His lips smack as he picks his teeth, fitting the full length of his index finger into the cave of his cheek to reach his molar, glazing it with a film of saliva. That same hand will collect my money.

Distracted, I fumble for my wallet and flip through a pocketful of loose coins. The newspaper clipping catches the wallet's leather flap and rides the air, landing on the gum display. The clerk's caught by surprise and snatches the clipping. I anticipate he'll give it back, but instead he reads the print. "Huh." His expression sours. "Bobby died?"

"*Excuse me?*" Change spills from my hand onto the vinyl tiling.

"Bobby. Real nice fellow." He leans in, as if he's speaking in confidence. "*A little quirky*." Then he straightens his stance. "I didn't realize he passed. Looks like the family dug up a decent photo. I almost didn't recognize him."

"You knew him?"

"You could say that. He was a regular. Used to come and buy a couple Instant Lotto tickets and a forty ounce. Too often if you ask me, but that's none of my business. I just sell."

"Yeah." I laugh. "Sounds like him."

"Whataya doing with the obit? He a friend of yours?"

"You could say that." I crack my wallet to retrieve my driver's license, point to the surname. "I'm his son."

He hovers over the counter to compare the photos, and then stares me up and down. "No shit? Didn't realize he had a kid. Sorry for your loss, man."

I shove my ID and the obituary between dollar bills for safekeeping. "It's all good. He wasn't much of a dad. Sounds like you knew him better than I did." I'm tempted to ask more questions but hold my tongue, fearful and embarrassed to expose how little I actually know.

He pushes the cashier drawer closed. "It's on me, man." Then he squats down, rips an Instant Lotto ticket from the roll. "Maybe you'll be luckier than he was."

He pushes a Lucky Street two-dollar scratch-off into the pile. If I match three like items I could win half a million dollars. The odds are slim to none, but I appreciate the deed.

"I hope so."

He returns my smile. There's comradery in the gesture.

"But, hey, ah...*thanks*. It means a lot."

He nods. With his obligation finished, he retreats to the break room.

21

JUNE, TWENTY-EIGHT YEARS OLD (PRESENT TIME)

The soiled porcelain shines against the fluorescent lights. My two hands grip the bowl, the seat lifted to widen the shooting range, my middle and pointer finger ready to trigger my gag reflex. I rattle remnants of food in my gut with a jig to prepare for an easy ride, but all that emerges is bile. I've reached a new low: a gas station bathroom.

Against its will, my stomach cramps to heave what it can find. Having consumed nothing but coffee, the vomit is mostly acidic, brown liquid with a few day-old undigested chunks, but my tightly wound nerves are determined to expel every last drop from the maze of my bowels.

There's no logical reason for forcing a purge. I haven't eaten today, there's no risk for weight gain. I can't lie and say I don't find pleasure in the chunks resurfacing, which would have been calories to burn, but the motivation lies in the comfort of the habit, the release. The addiction isn't the food. Not fully. It's the feeling of emptiness that comes when all is said and done.

The purge is a thought-out punishment, the chance to flirt with mortality and taunt my own soul by holding its body hostage. Perhaps most of all, it's a thrill. I loathe—and love—the high.

I wipe the bitter spit from the creases of my mouth and tap out a generous amount of pink soap, scrubbing until my hands are raw. My reflection stares back from the fractured mirror—a lean collarbone, atrophied biceps, and prominent cheekbones, more palpable than the year before. This girl is a stranger, a neglected version of the first thirty years.

"What's your problem?" I meddle, picking her flaws. They go beyond the superficial, deeper than oversized pores and under-eye circles, to her flaws in character—poor judgment, lack of self-control.

"Get your shit together." It's the same command on a different day. I slap my cheeks until they're hot, and then furiously rub to dull the sting. "Can't even make it one fucking day," I scold.

I yank a wad of paper towel to dry my face. The cheap material disintegrates onto my moist skin. I stare into the drain and imagine plummeting, free-falling into the sewage. The only difference between Anthony and me: we chose a different poison, and he managed to get sober.

There's a powerful knock on the door. Startled, I slip on the slick tile, smacking my elbow into the sink.

"June! You ready?"

The entire length of my arm tingles, but there's nothing to do but ride out the prickling sensation. My funny bone will soon form a bruise. "Will ya wait a minute?" I inspect the bowl's rim for splashed puke, then open the door.

"Good thing you're not the diabetic," I jab, eyeing the snacks.

He glares, annoyed, and then rotates his neck like he's on the lookout. The store is empty. Softly, he whispers, "That clerk. He knows my dad."

"What?"

He holds the obituary like a badge. "Can you believe it? My dad was a regular. Bought booze and lotto tickets."

To be honest, I'd forgotten about Robert's death. "Wow, small world."

"He didn't say much, but it was better than nothing." His eyes lower, hint disappointment. He places the clipping in his pocket. "He didn't know Robert had a son. I'm not surprised, but it would've been nice to be mentioned. People talk about things they're proud of. Guess that wasn't me."

I don't bother consoling. My words would be a clear attempt to hide what Anthony knows to be true. His dad only looked out for himself, and did a poor job at that.

He cracks the Pepsi. The carbonation releases a sizzle. "Hey ah..." He takes a swig. "What you said earlier. I, ah, I hate that I'm the destructive influence in your life." He inches closer, cornering me between the aisles of kettle chips and over-priced toilet paper. "All of this, seeing our past, this stuff with my dad, it got me thinking. Maybe our moments aren't done being made."

Our argument weighed on him. I didn't think he'd give it another thought. He never did before. It's a bold confession, one I've waited months to hear, but I'm exhausted.

"Why did you knock on my door, Anthony?"

He strokes my thumb, gently moving it aside, his fingers maneuvering to separate mine, the Chex Mix bag crinkling and slipping from his armpit's hold. "Because you're all I have."

"Anth." I shiver and cross my arms, slowing the advance but also hiding my assaulted, cracked knuckles. "I'll admit, there's a side of me that wants to wipe the slate clean, maybe even...I don't know...be *us* again. But it's nonsense and you know it. We can't exist as friends in the real world, let alone a couple." I step back. "I wish I knew God's plan."

He rolls his eyes, adamantly shaking his head. My elbow's bruised, but so is his ego. "This God you talk to all the time." His pitch raises, his voice now stern. "You've done it for as long as I can remember. God says this and God knows that. You wait for permission to do anything. You're like, you're like a toddler on the edge of a swimming pool. Dive in for once!"

"Anthony, stop. You're just hurt, I get it."

He ignores my plea. "Hell, I get that I can be oblivious, selfish even. I need to step out of my own head, but you need to step *into* yours. Figure out what *you* want. Take God off the pedestal and sit him next to you. Stop looking to the clouds and look in the fucking mirror."

I'm stunned. Of all the years we've known each other—shared a conversation, shared a bank account, shared a bed—he's never challenged my spirituality. It was always my thing.

"Listen." He steadies his breath, a practiced tactic to control a rising temper. "I'm sorry, if I..." He pauses. "Or, you know what, maybe I'm not."

"Excuse me?"

"Maybe I'm not sorry. Maybe I said I was sorry because on some subconscious level that's what society expects of a man who cheated, and I know that. I understand the game. If I outwardly express remorse, I'll be forgiven. Maybe someday I will be sorry, truly sorry. Maybe. But if we're laying it all out there, I'm confident that ending our relationship was the best thing I could have done, because if I didn't, *you would have never left me*. I did it the only way I knew how—by doing something so awful that you had no choice but to leave."

There's a pressure on my chest, no, more like a fist shattering my ribcage. Anthony may have cheated, but *I* filed for divorce to end the marriage for good. I hold ownership of that move. *I* had that power. If his cheating wasn't merely a bonehead lapse of judgment, but instead a step in his master plan, then that power is stripped from me.

His words are like a runaway train. "You always took me back," he continues. "Staying would have stunted my growth. I'd have no reason to be introspective, to explore what the hell I needed, and still need. And you know what? You don't want to admit it yet, but you're better off, too."

"Wow, well, you laid it out there, didn't you?"

My chest can't take another blow. I did come to that conclusion: I am better off, but I own that revelation. He has no right to it. "Still impulsive, I see."

He stays silent. I denied his advance and put him on the defense. Now, suddenly, he doesn't need me anymore.

"Anthony," I whisper, not because I care if I'm heard, but because a louder tone would cause my voice to quiver, and I don't want him to hear weakness. "You trample over whatever good thing comes into your life, but whatever you're seeking will never come once the guilt of your actions catch up to you. You will never enjoy it. Keep slamming doors in the faces of those you leave and no one will invite you back in."

He closes his mouth. He's said enough, and he knows it.

Point blank, I ask, "Why are you a dick?"

He awkwardly laughs, shrugging. "That's what I'm trying to figure out."

Blue smoke creeps into our peripheral view, trailing from a beat-up Honda Odyssey. We freeze, and then dash toward the exit, called by duty. Anthony goes first, scanning the parking lot for witnesses, while I toss the restroom key on the counter.

Anthony removes the nozzle from the tank and I hop inside. Olivia is trembling, trying to contain the writhing jewelry box. Her palm's eye is wide open, wildly in search of its jeweled companion, but unlike before, they're not connecting. There's been no delivery. Olivia releases a primal moan. Her grimacing face is proof the warning was warranted. Anthony joins us inside and slams the sliding door. "What's going on?"

Olivia squirms, unable to find relief. The eye's majestic pinwheels of color suddenly transform into violent, ice-blue flames, the hottest of all. I pin down her forearm. Her muscles contract to restrain the eye's strength.

"Where's the coaster?" Anthony's arm thrashes through loose trash like a machete.

"Never mind that!" Olivia moans. "If the jewelry box wants me to suffer, I'm not backing down. *Let me feel this.*"

"You're fucking crazy!" he yells, and then turns away, skittish as the skin encasing the eye peels and curls.

Olivia gazes into the eye like a looking glass. Her free hand uses mine as a stress ball, her nails puncturing my knuckles. The smell is unbearable. I plug my nose but it does nothing. The sting of sulfur from Olivia's burnt arm hairs seeps into my nostrils. With the contents already purged, my stomach cramps and violently rouses whatever digestive juice is left.

Olivia gasps, and through watering eyes, I see why.

Within the dilated pupil, the outline of a home takes shape, then, before it, two floating bodies. Fiery tongues lash the home, doubling in number until they're all that's seen. A blood-curdling scream travels through the flames: the cry of a young girl.

Then the image disappears. Olivia collapses into her chair, heavily breathing as the pain subsides. She's drenched, as if she just stepped out of the shower, wrinkles guiding streams of sweat.

"Shh, it's OK. You're OK. Easy." I use the water bottle as a cold compress.

There is no need to have lived the moment to know what we saw. A fire took my great-grandfather's life. The eye just gave us a glimpse into a pending trip, and the very instant that, as a young girl, Olivia's soul gained consciousness.

Spooked, Winston cowers in the van's cargo space. But when I look around, Anthony is gone.

I slide the door open and find him on the curb, gnawing his nails down to the quick. He sees me and stands. There's a cold listlessness in his eyes, as if he's suddenly detached from the life around him.

Is it the gore of Olivia's incident that got to him? Or our unresolved conversation, violently interrupted by a fiery omen? Maybe it's both.

"You comin'?" Olivia calls from the van. It's the question we should be asking her, but within seconds, her ponytail is smoothed and her two signature white strips of hair are back in alignment.

He nods twice, but keeps his head down. His arm is slung across his chest and grips his neck, a gesture used for protection. Anthony returns to the driver's seat and puts the van in drive. He doesn't bother fidgeting with the radio.

When he stops for oncoming cars, an Oldsmobile Bravada pulls into fuel pump four. Inside is a young mom with her toddler son snug in the backseat, occupied with *Green Eggs and Ham*. She fumbles for her credit card. I envy her afternoon running errands, oblivious to secret portals and magic hands. Traveling faster than the speed of light is exhilarating, but living in the dark is easy, comfortable. It's hard to miss what isn't known.

"June," Olivia calls, the eye suffocated in a clenched fist. "Where's my Little Debbie?"

Shit. I forgot. "I, I'm sorry, Aunt Ol, I..." I stutter with guilt, but Olivia starts to laugh.

"You owe me one."

Anthony pulls into the street and quietly takes orders from Olivia, who navigates the back roads of Detroit.

My reflection finds me again, this time in the van's smudged, distorted wing mirror. My irises project. Swirls of amber and chestnut bleed into sage green. Though dull in comparison to the lucent neon jewelry box we've become accustomed to, they are still beautiful. This girl's familiar. This girl I know. I stare directly into the girl's eyes, *my eyes*, and ask, *God, are you listening?*

22

ANTHONY, TWENTY-EIGHT YEARS OLD (PRESENT TIME)

The house is a dump. Blades of grass fill fissures in the concrete. Paint-chipped vintage advertisements line the home's exterior. One window is patched with the cardboard left from a Vernors soda box, sealed with layer after layer of duct tape. The lawn is a car graveyard, showcasing the rusted tombstone of a once grand El Camino.

"Here we are," Olivia proclaims. I roll up to the curb.

"Is it safe?" June's wary. I am too. Even if it's not haunted, it should be condemned.

"Not that one. That's Sam's house. The lot next to it."

June lowers the window. "There's nothing there."

"I know," she says smartly, then unfastens her seatbelt. "It burned down."

The door slides open before the van's in park. Olivia staggers off her seat, landing on the pavement with a grunt. Winston follows, heeling at her ankles, his feather-duster tail sweeping the loose gravel.

June stores the jewelry box in her purse and prepares to exit. I'm expected to join, but my tense grip cements on the steering wheel.

"Wait." My heart punches my ribs. My airway constricts, adding pressure to my chest. I know this feeling. I thought I'd walked it off. Fuck. I only suppressed it temporarily. *Fuck.* I'm having a panic attack.

"What are you waiting for?" June asks. Her facial features disintegrate, piece by piece, until all that's left is a peach-toned fog.

The click of the automatic lock echoes like a shotgun. "Give me a minute."

"We don't have time, Anth. Come on." She's halfway out, one foot on the ground.

"Wait!" I beg.

She stops. Time stops. Spit floods my cheeks. Vertigo sets in. I swallow furiously and find a point of focus, praying the spinning stops.

"Anthony." The voice is distance, screamed from the bottom of a canyon. "Can you hear me, An..." The words fade out, replaced by a high-pitched, continuous ringing.

"ANTH!"

With force, my neck jerks sidewise and repetitively cracks, a sound like a shoe crushing bubble wrap. June's fingers squeeze my jowls, pinching the tender skin against my teeth. Blood trickles onto my tongue. The metallic taste jars me, as does a firm slap, curing my symptoms like the shake of an Etch A Sketch.

She's suspended over the console, her upper body inside the van, supported by her core while her feet stay firmly planted on the ground. Her abdominal muscles tremble and eventually cave, causing her hands to fall onto the safety of the seat cushion for support.

I collapse into the steering wheel. "June, I never want to see that again," I mutter, lips on leather. My vision's cleared, but my breathing accelerates.

"See what again?" Shaking, she settles into the passenger seat. "What are you talking about?"

"What if the guide doesn't show?" I snap. "Are we going to sit here and watch Olivia die? She nearly fried to death, June, right in front of us, *in my fucking van*, and there was nothing we could do to save her." My speech is frantic, a bull-rushing stream of consciousness. "I keep waiting for some glorious revelation, but around every corner is another dead end. And what happens when this is over? I've lost everything, June—Aunt Elaine, my dad, and now, *even you*."

Cancer took Aunt Elaine in January, one month after the diagnosis returned as triple negative breast cancer. That was my last panic attack, sprawled on an exam table surrounded by eggshell-white walls, the tissue paper crinkling with the slightest move while Aunt Elaine—the *real* patient—sat contently in the plastic chair and learned of her options. "Your tumor cells lack the necessary receptors that respond to common treatments. You may respond to chemotherapy, but I must disclose, we caught this late..." She was fifty-three years old, approaching her golden years when she'd finally be free to care for *herself*. How did Aunt Elaine feel before her death? Where was *her* jewelry box?

"I don't have the answers either." June's voice cracks, desperate. "I'm *terrified*, Anthony, but I keep going back to what Lenny said: 'The jewelry box seeks the three of you.' We have to believe that. I *choose* to believe that."

"I thought maybe I'd learn something about my dad," I continue, overriding her plea. "Something redeeming, like he was a secret philanthropist or fed starving kids. I dunno, *anything*. But according to the clerk, he was exactly what he came off as—a drunk."

"Stop!" It's a primal yell, exhausting her lungs of air. "I've spent my entire life believing in God out of fear." Her eyes lock onto mine. "You said it yourself, I depend on Him, I can't make a decision without a consultation, but what if my perception of God is what's holding me back? What if Olivia isn't the only one of us that needs reminding? What if, intuitively, we've known what God is all along, but just forgot? We must keep going. We have to *try*. If nothing comes of this, the effort was sure as hell better than being stagnant, because if I find out when it's too late that paradise was before my eyes this entire time, I'm going to be pissed that I didn't wake the fuck up." Her lids squint, narrowing piercing eyes, which for the moment are indistinguishable from Olivia's. "You will get your shit together, Anthony, because this time, yours isn't the only soul at stake."

Her rebuttal is unexpected. Though we disagree, at times I was envious of her relationship with religion. Her unwavering faith has always been the ace in her pocket. Her safety net when pitted against the unknown, giving her a pass to relax: Jesus take the wheel, everything happens for a reason, God willing, *inshallah, im yirtzeh hashem.*

A rustling of grass puts June on alert. "Shh," she silences me, keen to the sound. I spot Olivia and Winston to our left, gazing at an empty lot and nowhere near the noise. It's not them.

In the distance, a pattern of footsteps is heard, growing louder as they approach. June looks to me for help.

A woman's voice speaks: "Why didn't you page me?"

23

JUNE, TWENTY-EIGHT YEARS OLD (PRESENT TIME)

Two shiny patent leather high heels sink into the dirt, supporting bone-thin legs clothed in nylon. "Things would have been much easier if you'd messaged. It's such a hassle to wait on others. I didn't keep you, did I?" The voice is melodic, soprano in range, projecting from a trained diaphragm. "Olivia surely was in awful, awful pain. The eye doesn't go easy before the sixth trip."

The jewelry box radiates with each syllable spoken, its light peeking through my purse's seams.

Cautiously, I turn. She wears a dark green pencil skirt, perfectly pressed and paired with a stark white button-down shirt topped with a wing-tipped collar that nicely complements satin gloves. Tightly spiraled curls fall from her scalp like ribbons from a bow. Her outlined lips are ruby red and freshly glossed. I would guess she's in her early seventies, but she carries herself with the zest of youth.

My expression must scream fear. Her head tilts with empathy. "Don't be afraid, dear. You've made it this far, haven't you? And young man." She beckons Anthony with two swift claps. "What's wrong with you? You reek of body odor."

The steering wheel glistens with Anthony's sweat. He's hyperventilating into cupped hands.

"Now, now. Repeat after me." One at a time, she lifts her fingers. "One, two, three. Very good. And again: one, two, three." Anthony bobs his head while counting in unison. "Good, dear. See, you're OK. The attack will pass. Keep counting. There's no use worrying about what you can't control." Like a spell has been cast, his tense shoulders lower.

She drags a canary yellow scarf from her blouse and waves it in the air. "Yoo-hoo! You must be Olivia. Over here, please." Her ankles shake as her heels sink deeper into the grass.

Aunt Ol shades her eyes from the sun, unsure what to make of this fanciful, persistent woman.

"I knew we'd meet eventually, but never did I think it'd be so long!" She speaks to Aunt Ol like an old acquaintance, with exuberance, curls dangling. "I'm so glad Lenny found you. He is such a gentleman, doing me a favor like that. What a sweetheart." She curtsies like a queen. "It's a pleasure."

"Who the hell are you?" Aunt Ol looks as if she's seen a ghost.

"Of course, of course. Can't forget pleasantries." Her flute-like laugh prompts a wood thrush to sing. "Meira. Meira Schreiber."

"I'm not here to play games, Martha. We have business to take care of—"

Meira continues a one-sided conversation. "I hope you enjoy the grounds. I've done my best, but being that it's just me, two lots are a tremendous burden. Much different from your childhood, I'm sure. Nothing lasts forever. Now, come along!" She stomps toward the boarded-up house next door and climbs the uneven porch stairs. At the top, she realizes she's alone.

The van door slams. Anthony yanks his pants above his gut and walks toward the house, noticeably more self-composed.

"Did you change your mind?" I whisper as he passes.

"What do we have to lose?" he argues. "Like she said, why worry about what we can't control?"

I should be pleased, but disturbed feels more appropriate. Just like that, Anthony's gained a new mantra and drank this woman's Kool-Aid.

Winston's next, waddling through the forest of weeds, enticed by the call like the children of the corn.

"Ah very good," Meira squeals. Winston's moist nose kisses her shins. "Why hello, sweet feline. You have a healthy appetite, I see." She pats Winston's head barely hard enough to bend his hairs. "The remaining two can see themselves in." She speaks of Olivia and me. "Don't be putzy. That eye you've sprouted may be wise, but trust me, the circumstances around it can be rather ghastly."

Olivia's dumbfounded or peeved—it's tough to tell—with one hand on her hip and the other curled into a fist. She takes a final glance at the empty land, then meets me on the sidewalk. "This lady better not be a crock of shit." She makes it one step, then advises in a low, uncompromising tone. "Don't take the jewelry box out until I say so."

Together we approach the front door.

The door flies open before we can knock. Meira greets us with a silver platter of assorted cookies, all doused with powdered sugar. Behind her, the table is set with four miniature dessert bowls with luster edging and hand-painted roses and accompanied by four pearl-white napkins ringed with sterling silver. Olivia takes a cookie while I watch, and I can't help but feel the heat of Meira's gaze.

"Not hungry?" she asks, taking the plate around to Anthony.

I shake my head.

"I see. Well, please sit. I'll pour you a glass of water. Surely you'll agree to improve your hydration." She disappears into the kitchen, which is sectioned off from the dining room by a swinging door, humming a dulcet melody.

The house smells of mildew. The foyer is bare, not even a coat rack, and the dining room table is leveled with an outdated *Encyclopedia Britannica*. The home is a bleak comparison to Meira. It seems the polished beauty lives with the unkempt beast.

She returns, balancing three crystal glasses of water filled to the brim. They spill on the unvarnished tabletop as she lowers the haul. "I didn't forget!" She darts to the kitchen and returns with a porcelain teacup for Winston.

Olivia pushes the water aside. "We want answers. Who are you?"

Meira sets a napkin on the table and tidies the spill.

"There. If we take good care of our things, they'll serve us well. Another cookie?" She lifts the plate to Anthony.

Olivia slams her fist on the table, causing the broken leg to slide off its temporary fix. Three waters and a teacup crash to the floor. Olivia doesn't flinch. Neither does Meira.

"I told you, Olivia. My name is Meira Schreiber."

"That means nothing to me."

"It certainly means something to me."

"What are you doing here?"

"I live here, of course."

"Sam lives here."

"Sam *lived* here. I bought it."

"Is he...?"

"Dead? Yes. He lived a long life. Turned eighty-five the day before the widowmaker took him. Wonderful man. We grew quite close at the end." The news slows the ping-pong of conversation.

"He was." Olivia bows her head and then opens her hand for the first time since the image appeared. "What do you know about this?" The lid furiously flutters, as if it had reached the surface for air.

In an uncontrolled, seemingly uncharacteristic fashion, Meira jumps to her feet. Aware of her brashness, she dusts her crisply pressed skirt and finds her seat. "Its beauty never ceases to amaze me, and it's different each time. Just like our fingerprints, I suppose."

"Do you see these often?" Anthony asks with his mouth full. He nibbles a pistachio-cream cookie.

"It's a family business, you could say." Meira scoots her chair closer to Olivia. Her tranquil voice reminds me of my mother's, the same sweet tone that'd read me Bernstain Bear books while I dozed off to sleep. Softly, reassuringly, she whispers, "I will tell you all you need to know."

24

OLIVIA, EIGHTY-EIGHT YEARS OLD (PRESENT TIME)

The house is a time capsule trapped in 1940s fashions. I'm sucker-punched with nostalgia. The stairwell is as I remember, with the square-edged, unadorned balusters expected in a Tudor Revival. The botanical wallpaper, the same wallpaper my mother envied and my father mocked, clings to dried-out glue and peels from decades of humidity's abuse. I helped Sam's mom mark his height on the wall beside the fireplace, always generous with the measuring to solicit a toothless grin. Though a few years younger, he was eager to surpass me and, thanks to second dinner helpings, quickly did.

Meira floats to a solid oak cabinet that stretches to graze the near ten-foot-tall ceiling. Its glass is fractured into thirds. Stored inside is a solid row of hardcover books. She recites titles as she scans their spines: "*Dhammapada*, *Arul Nool*, *Talmud*, *Qur'an*, *King James Bible*, *Gospel of Thomas*, *I Ching*...ah! Here it is!"

She frees a maroon cover with gold leaf ornamentation, hand-bound and hinged with two metal clasps. It's easily three-inches thick, an antique kept in pristine condition, only the yellowed pages hint to its age. It smacks the table with a *bang*. Block letters read: *Phoenician History*.

"What's this?" Anthony cracks the cover, examining thin pages edged in gold. Meira cringes watching sugar seep into the binding and reaches her breaking point when he licks his finger to turn the page.

She spares the book from a sticky assault. "Do you wish to see the best part?"

Anthony nods. She staggers the pages like a deck of cards, and as she does, an image takes shape—mesmerizing greens, blues, and reds. A silver, metallic lining forms five vertical pillars of varying heights, a round circle as their base, and in its center a smaller oval. "Beautiful, isn't it? Always there but frequently missed, unless one takes the time to search."

June's first to acknowledge the shape. "It's a...hand?"

Elated, Meira affirms. "Yes, my dear! Indeed it is. What else do you see?"

June stands for an aerial view. Meira flattens the pages to sharpen the details. "Look familiar?" Her flawless, straight teeth spread ear-to-ear, a mouth that shuns coffee and turns its nose up at wine.

She requests my hand. I intend to resist, but before I can decline, the palm's eye finds Meira and smiles back. Not in the conventional sense—it doesn't have a mouth to do so—but it stares with adoration, like a mother looking into the eyes of her nursing infant, and for a moment, the pain subsides.

The comparison is undeniable—two almond-shaped eyes dazzling with indescribable pigments of color, perfectly set within wrinkled palms. Even my superficial veins mimic the drawing's aesthetic embellishments. My hand is the manifestation of the book's hidden secret.

"Of course, there are some differences," Meira points out. "Yours is a splendid shade of blue, whereas this one has a touch of red."

There's an innocence to June, an inquisitive nature I've not seen since she was a child, when she'd crawl onto my lap and inquire about the moles on my cheek or why my leathered skin was not as soft as hers. Age beats that out of us, but now those same, curious eyes look to Meira.

"Why is Olivia's blue?" she asks.

Meira delights in the question. "Because of the depth of her soul, my dear. Blue is the color of the unknown. The greener bits show her growth, and the streaks of indigo are divinity peeking through. The indigo is new. It appeared when she bridged the gap between the finite and infinite."

"Infinite? You mean, God?"

Meira thinks for moment, her finger filling the dimple in her chin, then decides, "If that's what you wish to call it."

She flips to a bookmarked page.

Once again, there's a drawing of an eye, but with a menacing quality that brings a dark sense of unease. It's a gaze I'd rather avoid.

"The evil eye!" Meira proclaims robustly. "The malevolent glare. The curse that's haunted humanity since the dawn of time, given to unsuspecting victims to wish them harm or misfortune."

"The what?" June's curiosity turns to apprehension.

"The evil eye," Meira repeats, indifferent to the concern. She catches on when June skids from the table.

"Oh, I see! You think the eye on Olivia's palm is evil. Oh no, dear girl, quite the contrary. The evil eye we see here is a symbol of life's unexplained, unfortunate events. It's simpler for our brains to rationalize, you see, when we have an object of reference. Some sort of entity to blame, don't you agree? But Olivia's newly formed eye is equipped to protect *against* evil and is guarded by the prestigious, very rare manifestation of the hamsa."

"*That's* what Lenny meant," I interject. "When he said the eye was held within the security of my palm."

Meira smiles, a confirmation. "When we fall, our hands protect us from the crash, and that's what the hamsa came to do. By nesting within your palm, your soul became fearless, ready to revisit devastating moments from your past to observe their significance. This time with the advantage of maturity."

Again, she flips the page and lands on an image of a man, eyes closed in meditation, with a third eye positioned between his brows.

"Inside Olivia's palm is the third eye, the eye of enlightenment, that sees beyond our worldly senses," she explains. "Lenny informed you of this, no? He said he would. I would have done it myself had I not been stuck in traffic. I-75 is just appalling at rush hour. Anywho, the hamsa is only given to those who have brushed with death. It is quite an honor, if one can stomach the incident that earned it—war heroes, refugees, cancer survivors—oh, it's dreadful what one goes through to qualify. It's the universe's consolation prize. But for the survivor, there is no guarantee the payoff is worth the trauma. It's all in the eye of the beholder, I suppose."

"No shit." The thought slips out, and I'm awestruck with the irony that my father's death—the event that triggered my life's pursuit of greater knowledge of divinity, the event I've held in contempt—simultaneously held clues to the answer.

But something else she said lingers. She referred to me, and those like me, as a *survivor*. When I was younger, I was labeled a victim. *Poor Olivia, the victim of such a tragedy*. But I refused to hear it. To me, it was condescending and connoted weakness. A victim is acted on, but the word *survivor* conjures strength. A survivor governs their potential, not only to exist, but to prosper. *That* is a title I can embrace.

Meira places the book before June. "Sweet girl, will you flip to the chapter I have marked?" June hesitantly agrees. "That's it, yes, stop. Be a doll and read to us."

She begins. "The hamsa, also known as the khamsa, the Hand of Miriam, the Hand of Fatima, and the Hand of Mary, is an ancient amulet used for protection from the evil eye. The origins point to the Phoenician goddess, Tanit, in the ancient city of Carthage on coastal Tunisia."

June stops and with a wrinkled brow asks, "Who are the Phoenicians?"

Meira fervently clarifies, "Phoenician colonies dotted the Mediterranean Sea in modern-day Lebanon, Israel, Gaza, Syria, and Turkey, but also spread as far as Africa. Fascinating culture, truly fascinating, and not given proper credit, if you ask me."

"Oh," June accepts the answer with reserve, obviously in over her head. Meira smiles, satisfied, and nods for June to continue.

"Tanit ruled over the sun, stars, and moon, and was worshipped as a symbol of fertility. When a Phoenician woman could not bear a child, or the child was born ill, she was thought to have encountered the cursed gaze of the evil eye. Tanit was depicted lifting an open hand, and the Phoenicians, being seamen and traders, took amulets of the symbol on their travels. Eventually it transformed into the hamsa, the protection against all evil..."

June's voice blends into white noise. The eye's effect on my body has been euphoric since it found Meira. My senses are hyper-aware of miniscule details.

Dust falls into the window's light and dances like rebellious fireflies fighting their nocturnal nature and creating an aura around Meira. Behind her is a multi-panel window with repeating diamond shapes framed in polished timber. It's the window my mother found us under, wrapped in a blanket heavy with soaked blood, trapping the heat needed to survive. I have not time traveled; I am here, in this moment, but the image is as strong as it was at fifteen.

A harsh revelation strikes me: that a memory is more painful than reliving the past. When an original moment happens, it simply *is*. It is an unadulterated, unspoiled event. We are consumers processing but not yet comprehending the significance the singular moment has on our timeline. It is later that hindsight brings pain and a yearning for what was lost. That yearning plagues the mind with attempts to rationalize what cannot be changed. We are tortured until we can let go of the need to control what was not ours to begin with, for we do not own, we experience. The jewelry box has us experiencing the original moment, just as we did the first time. I need not be afraid.

Meira catches my detached stare. "Olivia. Interesting, don't you think?"

I manage half a smile.

She's taken over the role of informer, teaching from memory and not a textbook. "Phoenicians were extremely influential.

Their leader, Hiram of Tyre, helped furnish King Solomon's first temple in Jerusalem. It was destroyed twice, but the ruins are the foundation for the Temple Mount, and its neighboring Western Wall, a deeply spiritual site for Jews, Muslims, and Christians." Her flimsy, gesticulating wrists find me. "You've been there, right, Olivia?"

"How do you know that?" I'm caught by surprise. I've never come into contact with this woman. I have not told her that's where the jewelry box fell into my lap. In fact, she has not seen the jewelry box at all. It's hidden in June's purse.

"Just a hunch." She smirks. "You seem like a worldly lady keen on adventure. Surely you wouldn't travel without visiting such a place." When she speaks, she does not blink. Her eye contact is strong and holds until its recipient breaks.

A familiar rattling startles Winston, who's curled in a ball under June. Meira grins.

"Is it time?" she asks.

June stiffens and waits for my approval.

"Actually," Meira adds lightly, while individually loosening the finger slots on her gloves, "I don't think it's up to you."

The jewelry box violently trembles and shoots from June's purse. Winston springs into my lap for safety as it tumbles across the floor, unhinged as a rabid animal. It's the strongest and fiercest reaction from the jewelry box we've seen yet.

"What will it do to her?" June cries, using her crossed arms as a shield.

Meira balances on her knuckles and hunches over the table like a perched gorilla. "It will remind her!" She's yelling over the box's irrepressible clatter. "She will see her origin and her destiny. The peace of the universe depends on her soul, just as it depends on *yours*."

My muscles succumb to the magnetic force, which lures my arms without consent and drags my body with them.

Meira kneels before the jewelry box. It calms with her approach. Gently, she taps each opal gemstone. They immediately transform to the familiar, vibrant blues. A solid beam of light rockets toward the ceiling and flails like an industrial searchlight.

A field of tranquility, thick as a curtain, encases the table. "Ease your worries, dear," Meira assures. "You have not been forgotten."

She flicks the lid.

A spinning pendant rises, then suspends in mid-air. A sterling-silver brooch in the shape of a sunflower revels in the radiant light. It's *my* brooch. The one I bestowed to the Muslim boy in Jerusalem.

"Wonderful." Meira is beaming. "Your gift has found its way home. Before his death, the young man made a wish, requesting that it continue on adventures."

"He passed?" I ask, alarmed. He would be only in his thirties.

"Yes. Rather senseless, I'm afraid. Killed by a stray bullet walking home from the mosque. His soul crossed quickly. He was full of prayer before the bullet struck his heart, just having come down from transcendence."

There's a pinch on my heart, as if a wedge was severed with the news. This young boy I met in passing has become an integral part of my story. Somehow, I hope he knows.

With a snap of her fingers, Meira splits the beam. The splintered light quests for June and Anthony's chests, but then opts for my palm's eye, my third eye, just as it's done all along. The jewelry box has been the vessel that cabs the tagalong souls, but this time the burden is lightened, and I see that the light has fused with Meira's palm as well. She shares the load.

As their souls surge, I do not sense Anthony's indignation or June's apprehension. What I sense is indescribable, but if I were to try, I'd take the warmth of a spring sun toasting winter skin, the second sip of whiskey when the buzz sets in, and the guitar riff from a song so good, you're forced to shut up, close your eyes, and listen. Yes, that's it. I would take all of that and bottle it up, but even then something would be missing. This feeling is pure *love*.

Meira presides before the jewelry box, and with rehearsed mastery recites the familiar poem:

Our eyes can capture wonders, flashes of sublime.
Eternity surrounds you, irrelevant is time.
But darkness casts its shadow; evil we can't neglect,
For all that we encounter, is all we must accept.
For souls escape and race the light to another dimension.

25

OLIVIA, FIFTEEN YEARS OLD (SEVENTY-THREE YEARS AGO)

January in Michigan is brutal. Known for dark days, desolate neighborhoods, and cocooned families. With temperatures reaching single digits, this year is exceptionally ruthless.

The streets are covered with a knee-deep layer of fresh snow and two to three inches still to come. We live in a modest, drafty bungalow in Poletown, just shy of nine hundred square feet. The chipping blue paint on the 1920s wood siding makes it the eyesore of St. Aubin Street. My father had intentions to repaint the exterior but never got around to it, which goes against his borderline obsessive-compulsive tendencies and pride. But after overhearing my mother whisper about the urgency for a family budget, it makes sense. Built during the housing boom, it's a cookie-cutter replica of the one next door, and the one next to that. Our yard is too small to throw a baseball from end to end, but it's a roof over our heads, as my father says.

My father was among the Eastern Europeans who emigrated from Gdansk, Poland to America, eventually planting roots in Detroit for steady factory work. He stood shoulder to shoulder in a cramped cargo ship at fourteen, waiting in line for the next meal, only to vomit off the deck when the waves hit. From what I can gather, he came alone. He never spoke of his life before my mother, romantically claiming that it didn't start until he saw her face. When he had a few too many vodka and cranberries, he'd get teary-eyed reminiscing about Poland, changing to his native tongue and leaving us lost on the details.

He sits in the living room, now in his fifties, rummaging through the latest *Free Press* in an oversized, leather chair. Though I cannot remember the specific time frame, seemingly overnight my father's jet-black hair morphed to a salt-and-pepper mix. His beard turned first, gradually settling into a pleasant silver gray. Once the spitting image of Orson Welles, he's often complimented on his beard's robust thickness and manicured shape. His nose is rosy with bulbous lumps that distort its shape, the texture of an orange peel—a condition called rhinophyma, we were told. His bifocals magnify the irises of his eyes, making them disproportionate to his face.

"Olly-boo." He snaps the newspaper to smooth the creases.

"Yes, Pops?" The moisture from my breath generates a visible fog. It's just us tonight. Mom took Dorothy to Hudson's for a new dress, despite my father's grumbling, using this weekend's winter choral concert as an excuse. I'm wrapped in a blanket on the sofa, a human golabki, attempting to crochet but failing miserably. The metal hook stings my fingertips, frozen from the dropping temperature, so I toss them aside and sink into the blanket's cove, curling into a tight ball to form an impenetrable hotbox.

"Alright, that's it." He retucks his flannel shirt in three swift moves, then reaches for his steel-toed boots.

"What're ya doing?" I ask, my voice muffled by the fabric.

"Can't take it any longer," he answers, patting the pockets of his coat for gloves. "Going to stoke the coal furnace." He runs through a mental checklist: "Gloves, hat, shovel." Stubby fingers button his double-breasted wool coat. He's meticulous; his shirt sleeves always cuffed, shoes tightly laced, and overalls securely hooked. Always.

The door slams, followed by squeaks from the friction of boots on freshly fallen snow. The noise dulls as the distance grows. He's going to the coal reservoir in the garage. The cellar door bangs, once, then twice, bouncing from gravity's force. He must have his hands full and no patience to be gentle. Heating our home is backbreaking work. I peek out the window. He's on his second trip. The snow's too high for the wheelbarrow, so instead he carries the coal like he's cradling a baby, and it's equally as precious. The coal truck unloaded what was supposed to be half a winter's worth in November, but we're burning through it fast.

I slide down the cushion to form a reading cove. Shuffling through a stack of *LIFE* magazines, I find the *Harper's Bazaar* buried underneath. The model wears thick-rimmed sunglasses. A satin scarf wraps her towering hair, and tan arms knot it in place. Mom claims couture is for the egotist, but I don't see narcissism. I see sophistication and enviable elegance. As the publication touts, *Harper's Bazaar* is for "well-dressed women with well-dressed minds." Mom needs to relax.

A chill travels my spine, breaking my focus. "*Brr*!" I mutter, but the reaction doesn't fit the feeling. It's a tingling sensation, more like pins and needles than a shiver. "It's fuh-*reezing*." There's no use complaining. No one is listening. I free my hand to turn the page, but first, just for a moment I stop, acutely aware of the quiet, the stillness of winter. The house is empty, and the weight of the snow suppresses the movement of the tree branches, a straightjacket unyielding to wind. Faintly, the subtle rasp of a metal shovel digs into a pile of coal. Pieces clink against the cast iron.

Unexpectedly, a violent *boom* rattles the house.

My body hurls forward, smashing my ribs against the sofa's armrest. Whiplash bangs the rear of my head against the wall. My eyesight blurs.

My kidneys, punched during the blow, radiate pain down my lower back. Warmth expands from my crotch, reaching my knees; I involuntarily wet myself. The magazine's clutched into a paper accordion. The power of the vibrations shook the house floor. The door to the corner cabinet, where our good china is kept, is flung open. Two salad plates are shattered into sharp, glossy specks. What the hell just happened? My head throbs, but the pain takes a back seat to fear.

I snap to my senses, toss the blanket, and stumble to the side door, the same door my father passed through moments earlier. The eruption came from outside. Or was it the basement? I can't tell. Dust clouds the air, filling my lungs from every direction, blocking me from going further. I hear the crackle of ash after a fire, but can't see the flames, only blinding, suffocating smoke.

My body fights back with a violent cough. I'm craving oxygen but each breath feels like a lit wick traveling down the length of my esophagus, inching toward the dynamite. My chest burns. One hand presses my sternum for stability, and the other covers my mouth, trying to filter the air. Unable to bear it, I go inside and slam the door.

The reality sets in. I'm manic, swinging the door open without a thought to the consequences. The heat from outside hits my skin, a feeling like standing too close to a campfire. There's no question I've suffered burns, but just like a fingertip that first touches a hot iron, my nerve endings have not yet recognized the pain. At the bottom of the cement stairs is the cellar's opening, both doors flung up with gray mushroom clouds billowing out. It's ground zero. The blast came from the coal furnace.

"Dad!" I scream with the little tone left that the smoke hasn't stolen. I'm desperate. I need to see his face, I need to know he's OK. *I need my father*.

I wave my hands to cut the thick air but the explosion's remnants are too much to battle. I'm once again forced to retreat.

Defeated, I slam my forearms against the wall with clenched fists. "Dad! Where are you?" Now sobbing, my knees give out. My oxygen-depleted body drops to the floor. I have never been drunk, but I've seen my father, and I imagine this is how it must feel: loopy, with no control of my balance or bladder. I struggle to stand.

The door is assailed with violent force. "Olly! Get out! Get as far away from the house as you can! Move!" my father hollers. He collapses onto the steps.

The urgency in his voice emboldens me to rise. From the window I spot his face, his complexion as dark as the cloud that engulfs him, as if slathered by tar. His bifocals are gone, a casualty of the blast. His coat's ripped open, the bottom singed by the sparks. Portions of the wool are dancing with flames, flickering yellows and gold.

He manages to balance on his knee. Blood droplets dot the white snow's blank canvas. Impatient, he hurls the door open and drags me onto the icy porch by the collar of my shirt. My knees skid against the rough surface, ripping the cotton cloth and exposing my flesh to the frozen ground.

"Go!" he shrieks. "Now!"

It's an urgent yell that only a father can give. Vehement, with no room for argument. He flees, returning to the fiery scene. Without looking back, I stammer down the side-stairs and slump into the unplowed snow. The cold is a shock, but it relieves the throbbing cuts. Like a soldier, I stay below the smoke and crawl toward the road on all fours until I reach the driveway. Shoveled this morning, it's a provisional bunker with a powdery barricade.

In the center of the front yard sits the base of a snowman, half melted yet poignant, like a once venerable statue abandoned in a city battered by war. My sister and father built him last week, and the persistent, bitter cold kept him alive. Hours ago, he was standing tall, topped with an old ascot cap.

"Oh my God, oh my God, oh my God..." A voice draws near. Quivering, of baritone pitch. With it the repetitive and quick-paced squeaking noise of boots stomping through wet snow. He spots me, dazed and motionless, with eyes wide open but a blank stare that exhibits no signs of comprehension. I'm indistinguishable from a tattered doll tossed on the floor when the child grows tired of playing.

"Olivia! Oh my God, please be OK." It's our neighbor, William. His cold hand compresses my neck. It feels good, comforting. I'm still.

A heavyset man, his breathing is labored. Perching over my head, I feel his panic in the trembling of his fingers pressed against my carotid artery. Then, it comes. I begin to sob. Hysterically sob. William's distress illustrates the horror of it all. He rolls me onto my back to examine the injuries.

William is a bank teller. His kids, Sam and Darlene, are eight and twelve. I see their shadows standing on the porch, observing what's unfolding.

He has no medical training but moves quickly. "Sam!" he screams. "Get the old shirts in the bottom dresser drawer in my bedroom. Go!" It is a desperate order. Sam hustles back inside, while Darlene stands frozen.

William doesn't waste time. He peels off his own shirt and begins wrapping my leg, looping it three times for a snug bandage. He finishes with a tight double knot, causing me to wince and howl. Sam returns with an armful of plaid, makeshift dressings.

"Put 'em here," William orders. "Make a pillow, son." His pudgy palm stabilizes my neck. "Olivia, listen to me. Was anyone else home with you?"

I want to scream "yes!" But the words don't form.

Again, he asks, "Olivia, please listen. Tell me. Is anyone else here?"

I'm shell-shocked. Sam takes over. He ties a second shirt over the gash on my knee. I mutter, "Dad...my..."

"There!" Before I can go on, Sam spots a figure emerging from the cellar. From the front, it is an abstruse, dark object covered in soot and coal. Smoke surges from the frame. It's my father. He stammers onward, slow and arduous steps. Finally, when the struggle becomes too great, he falls to his knees with a thud.

What's left of his jacket wouldn't cover a child, only charred flaps of cloth lay over his shoulders. Sparks jump from the metal clasps of his overalls. His hands are raw, clearly used to fight the blaze in an attempt to save the house, *in an attempt to save me*. William acts quickly, dropping the remaining shirts and running to my father's side. Sam stays with me.

"Stanley, roll! Snuff out the fire!" William doesn't wait. He hooks both arms under my father's armpits and drags him through the snow, using the elements to his advantage, then rolls him like a log. It works. Three or four rotations and the flames extinguish. But the damage is done. The overalls my father latched so tightly have melded together, making them impossible to remove. The hot material presses against his body and sears him like a branded calf.

"Good Lord, Stan," William weeps, barely recognizing his friend. "What can I...I mean, I, ah...what do I do?" he mumbles into blood-stained hands. He gags at my father's blistered skin, already peeling from his forehead, exposing shiny, fresh flesh underneath. Blisters form along on his cheekbones, swelling his face to twice its size.

A vehicle spotlights the battered men as if they are the leading characters on a stage. William's wife, Melinda, is driving their Oldsmobile —our substitute ambulance. My father's eyes catch the beam and reflect like those of a nocturnal critter—inanimate, but proof that *some* life remains.

"C'mon, Stanley, help me out. Let's go." William is not accustomed to manual labor, and lifting the dead weight of a two-hundred-pound man is beyond his capability. "Sam, lend a hand. Be gentle, son." Sam grabs for the pant legs while William handles his torso.

"Oh Stan...oh my...It's cleared for 'im." Melinda holds the door. She wears a floral pink nightgown with a puffy knee-length winter coat, complete with William's winter boots, which must have been closest to the door when she rushed to aid her husband.

I have a clear view into the car's cab. The men's efforts are successful. My father lays across the seat, head cocked and jaw dangling with no support from his neck. I monitor closely, watching his chest slowly rise and then fall, but the rhythm to which they shift up and down slows.

"*Turn at Warren.*"

"*No, Ferry's quicker.*"

Their contending voices determine the quickest route to the hospital. William gives one final command to his son before driving off: "Sam, take Olivia inside, but move her slowly. We may not be back tonight." The last sentence carries sadness, diffidence. Sam listens to his father like a private does to a corporal. I listen as well, but more for the inflection than the words delivered.

The vehicle reverses with a jolt, the jittery driver unpracticed behind the wheel, and then angles to face the road. A shadow shows William tending to my father, carefully stabilizing his head against the window so the small patch of hair that resisted the blaze is the only surface making contact with the glass.

I'm helpless. The severity of my father's injuries are ominous. As the car shifts to drive, I spot him in the window. My father's glacial blue eyes meet mine, and as they do, a rush of energy infiltrates my lungs, giving new life.

For an instant, peace flows from my core to my fingertips, and for the first time since the explosion, I take a breath. A breeze taps the wind chimes on the porch, the eerie notes like a church bell's toll, and I know, I just know, the makeshift ambulance is now a hearse. The vivid blues of those eyes burn into my memory, on his face an expression I'll never forget. The look of goodbye as a soul exits this realm.

Their car pulls away. The tail lights grow dimmer as distance grows. Heaviness in the pit of my gut confirms my suspicion, that this is the last time I will see my father.

"Olivia, are you alive?" Sam whispers, dusting the dirt from my forehead, dirt that hasn't seen the light since winter's start but is prematurely unveiled thanks to the fire's heat.

"Sam!" It's a young girl's voice. Long blond curls fall from a pink winter's cap, bouncing as she screams.

"Darlene! Go inside," he commands, playing the protective big brother.

"I'm scared, Sam!" Darlene's tiny fingers clasp the porch railings, chipmunk cheeks squeezed between the poles, her toes exposed to the ice. "Listen to me! We're fine, go inside!" Sam wraps the last flannel shirt around my scraped elbow. "Olly, blink once if you can hear me."

"I can hear you, Sam," I mumble, monotone.

"Can you move?" He's afraid to touch me. I save him the anguish and sit upright. "I'm, I'm sorry...I've never done this before." He scrambles to clear the snow, using his ungloved fists to shovel a pathway to his porch. "Is this OK?" His questions fall flat. "Please,

Olly!" He's begging, wiping tears and snot with his forearm, sniffling to restrain what hasn't fallen.

He cradles his knees and sways, a controlled hysteria. "I don't know what to do, Ol." Back and forth, back and forth, trapped in the rhythm, terrified to break tempo. "Your ol' man, is he...will he be alright?"

He makes a last-ditch effort to carry me, the words of his father echoing: "I'm trusting you with this." Just as he witnessed William do to my father, he hooks both arms under my armpits.

I'm entranced. Though the outside fury has died, I can see through our home's bay window that the smoke is thick, intermittently lashed with bright, fiery flames that juxtapose the winter's calm.

"Sam..." I quiver.

The flames multiply, crawling over one another for space, whipping the glass and thrashing the top rail of the window loose. A rumbling. The front door shakes as pressure builds.

"Sam!"

A loud *boom* hoists us through the air. Languid, we soar onto a snowbank ten feet from the blast, legs and arms tangled. The ice snaps my neck on impact, thrusting my skull forward with a fresh fissure. Sam hits the downward tilt of the bank. He somersaults twice before settling at the base.

The fire blends into Michigan's northern lights. A metallic warmth drizzles from my mouth, melting and pooling into the cool white snow. Yet, I'm not afraid. I don't bother to move. Instead I let the blood drain the life from my body. Calmly, I stare upward toward the glittering night sky, and passively look down upon my corpse. My feeble, mangled corpse. I see my heart stop.

Another, bolder light appears—a gaseous star without a concrete shape that overtakes the hemisphere. It's alluring, and like a snake I follow the charmer. Brighter and brighter it becomes, absorbing lightning, then wildly shooting bolts: a process of continuous self-regeneration. I realize that I too am lightning heading for its core, yet it keeps me at bay.

Doubt comes. Why can I not join? Am I worthy? But I know this is not true. I am worthy. I bask in its compassion and feel that I am enough. No expectations, no ulterior motives. All it desires is my company.

Suddenly, the illustrious star is struck with a great burst of light. It exuberates a renewed brilliance. In return, it spits a spark that falls toward the earth.

That spark absorbs into Sam, giving his skin a fluorescent glimmer that illuminates the night and then—*blink*—his eyes open, restored with life.

He makes a fist, then swivels his ankle. Stiffly, he lays on his side. On his hands and knees, he scoots up the snow bank but gets nowhere. The slick ice takes him back two steps for every one gained.

"Olly?" he cries. My ear is keen to his whisper, yet I'm still hovering above, close to the gaseous light. I want to answer, but cannot control my speech. Again, he tries to get my attention. "Olly, I'm coming." He digs his nails into the snow like spikes and grasps for my lifeless hand.

My view is 360 degrees—the light, the blaze, Sam, our home. Even land stretching hundreds of feet into the distance that follows the curve of the Earth. Neighborhoods down the block are calm, unaware of the turmoil. But that's how this works, the Earth oscillates chaos, giving reprieve to one area only to pummel another. Nothing is pardoned, for the natural law upholds justice. Whether for adversity or amity, we must wait our turn.

You will return. Go, a voice urges, but the language is vague. It's more of a thought, without speech, as if it came from within.

A subtle nudge urges me back. I return to my body, just as Sam did moments before.

I open my eyes. Sam's fingers intertwine with mine. When our palms touch, our souls once again race back to present time, but unlike previous trips, Sam's soul veers. It's slated for another destination. It won't be joining us.

26

JUNE, TWENTY-EIGHT YEARS OLD (PRESENT TIME)

The grandfather clock chimes four o'clock. It's of the Comtoise variety with a potbellied case and heavy, elongated pendulum, a popular furnishing throughout France for keeping time on the farm. Today, it welcomes back four vagabond souls.

Olivia's the last one to wake. She's groggy, nursing her forehead like she's tending a hangover. Each trip takes its toll. Her soul is weary.

"Where'd he go?" she asks. She speaks of Sam, her young neighbor and one-time savior.

Meira reapplies lipstick from a silver tube. "That's an excellent question." She curls her bottom lip to assure complete coverage while staying perfectly within the liner. "One that I don't know the answer to." She finishes with a lip-smacking pop.

"Then what good are you?" Unsatisfied, Olivia turns to mocking. "You're a guide. You're supposed to *know it all*."

Meira, remaining composed, puts the finishing touches on her blush. "That's absurd." She snaps the compact shut. "No one knows such things. I said I'd give you the answers you need. No more. No less. Sam's soul has left this world, but to where, I do not know. What I *do know* is he cannot return. Perhaps he's off to a parallel universe or rejoined the grand pool of energy." Her hands gracefully swirl, spinning at the wrists. "I fancy that idea the best. The jewelry box has limits. As long as your heart is still beating, your soul is restricted to travel within your present identity."

She discusses death like she's reporting the weather, acknowledging its unpredictability, but interested, nonetheless.

Stephen Hawking, the British physicist, collaborated with Thomas Hertog to publish a paper before his death on the controversial topic of multiuniverses. The theory claims the universe grew rapidly after the Big Bang with repeated bursts at speeds faster than light. During these bursts, small glitches in energy may have ballooned into larger pockets of space-time, creating alternate individual universes within an ever-expanding larger universe. Yet, with no way of testing their ideas, the paper remains theoretical, and the authors themselves were among the skeptics. It's too bad they didn't consult Meira.

"Identity?" I ask, unclear about the term's use.

"Yes, dear. An identity is who you consider yourself to be. Today you are June, tomorrow you are June, but after death will you be June?"

I shrug, unsure if her question is rhetorical.

She shrugs back. "Exactly."

"Your identity is a collection of moments experienced through the perception of June, and for the time being, houses your soul. Though temporary, they fit together perfectly. They *need* one another. Through your identity your soul gains wisdom, and through your soul your identity can *thrive*. You were meant to be June, so you are June, for now. These moments are stepping stones you hop along. The jewelry box doesn't go *back*' per se. It simply navigates your soul through the matrix of moments within the lifespan of your present identity."

Around the table, puzzled expressions reveal three minds straining to rationalize the concept, and not one of them successful. Even if her theory is correct, that souls can retrace points in an identity's life, the execution has yet to be explained.

"But how?" I press.

"The clue is in the opals. They are magnificent, are they not?" She nods to the jewelry box. "I think so, too. Opals are such precious gems, especially these. Now, an earthly opal acts like a prism. The light splits into the colors of the spectrum, then bends and bounces about the layers upon layers of spheres and gaps inside. Eventually, the assorted colors bounce back to the gem's surface for our eyes to admire."

I examine the detail of the gems. Just as Meira described, the color-pattern of each opal is in constant motion, creating a dazzling play of hues.

"And *these*," she continues. With a smile she polishes the gems. "These opals have special abilities. They split the waves of the souls that pass through. By doing so, we can simultaneously bounce about past, current, and future moments. But, as long as a beating heart calls for your identity's soul, that soul will return to its earthly origin. However, when your heart stops and the soul breaks free for good, it will rejoin with the light. But from there, where does it go? Well, we must wait and see."

Her white gloves are neatly stacked beside the resting jewelry box. They're in pristine condition. Not a speck of dust. She refits one, and then the other, when a flash of violet streams across the table. Meira's own third eye appears, radiating a lustrous, saturated amethyst glow. A secret she's shrewdly kept hidden.

"What is that?" Anthony leaps to his feet.

She continues pulling the satin over her wrists with meticulous care, like a doctor preparing for surgery. "Olivia can't have all the fun." She smirks, then rises to close sheer curtains to dim the day's light. "My dear Olivia."

Olivia's called to attention.

"I must say," Meira continues, "your brush with death may be one of my favorites. Wasn't it lovely? It's a bit selfish on my part, so insistently tracking you down, but I just can't help myself. It has a habit of revealing itself on the sixth trip, sometimes the seventh, but mostly the sixth. I make sure to have my conquests contact me just in case. I wouldn't dare miss it."

Meira leads. One by one we follow her to the table. Olivia is last to take a seat.

"What reveals itself?" I ask.

"The Unbound Love, of course. Did you not feel it? Like a parent rocking their child to sleep." She overlaps her arms and cradles thin air. "Or the first bite into a sufganiyot, my personal favorite. Have you tried? You must try. There's simply no dessert like it."

Anthony's eyes hang low. Meira's long finger lifts his chin. "The Unbound Love is like the pond in which the stones are set, or perhaps, the opal's silica spheres through which the light can pass, but it differs in the fact that it is discarnate," she explains. "Love surrounds all that we do. Surely you *felt* its presence, no?"

He turns away. "I guess a little, but at first I felt so...so."

"Empty?" Meira finishes.

He nods, surprised. "Yeah, exactly."

"It will come," she reassures. "A soul can attract love as the years go on, if you wish it to."

"Any idiot would wish for it." He pauses. Winston approaches to use his leg as a scratching post. Anthony stops to stroke his long fur, inciting a robust purr. "But, why can't I feel it now?" he asks.

"Because of the shield. When a soul first leaves its physical body, before surpassing the speed of light, it must first hurdle the Wall of Sentiment. It happens so quickly that we don't even notice. This wall is the embodiment of the emotions we have evoked in others. It appears, lovely Anthony, you have caused much pain. Though it is tempting to scream at the wall, release anger with reckless desperation at the injustices you've felt, in order to travel your soul must break through, and if you seek love when you cross, you must devote kindness while you live."

Winston stretches his neck. The slits of his eyes, glassy specks of chartreuse barely thicker than a nickel, stare at Anthony, revealing tiny portals to his soul. "By the sound of that cat you're off to a good start," Meira says.

Do onto others what you would have done to you. Love your

neighbor as yourself. Karma's a bitch. It's a cross-cultural golden rule, and apparently one worth following.

I'm suddenly heavy with guilt. I, too, felt loneliness on the last trip. Have I also caused pain? I'm not perfect. Silently, I recall my faults.

Meira clears her throat. "June, dear." She pushes the jewelry box aside then glides her fingers over my knuckles. I wince from the sting as she flakes the dry, cracked skin, a side effect from the purge. "The Wall of Sentiment reflects the treatment of *every* soul we encounter, including our own." It's a subtle reference. She knows my secret. I tuck my hands between my legs, ashamed.

Olivia's palm's eye begins to flutter. The teals and blues remain the dominant colors, but additional streaks of indigo and violet bleed through the iris. She flexes her wrist and plays with the shadows dancing on the ceiling. The eye is a flashlight in the tinted room. Olivia is notably calmer. Meira smiles, pleased.

She curls Olivia's fingers. "Let it rest." Once in a fist, Meira massages her forearm, which has bared the brunt of the strain. "Let me explain something, dear Olivia."

Olivia closes her eyes and indulges in the pampering.

"The seven trips come with a purpose. They are moments when your soul, or those who have joined your journey,"—she nods to Anthony and me—"were witnesses to suffering, tested by grief, or required to exercise empathy. Four of the trips are from *your* life's identity. These four trips helped build a strong moral foundation. Two trips are through the eyes of your accomplices, for they will later help spread the word, and one trip is for the soul that brought you stability, whose love for you never wavered, even when yours did. We cannot escape suffering in this life. *Embrace it.* The soul is a muscle. It must tear to be strengthened. These seven moments will prepare you for what's to come."

I silently recall our travels. Surely, revisiting my conversation with Michelle and Anthony reliving our wedding satisfies the requirement that two of the trips be through the eyes of accomplices. (*Michelle*. The thought of her jars me. Has she discovered that she, too, has value?

And, the spirit of life that was briefly within her, is it now freed from the stress of Michelle's heavy heart?) Then there is Jacoby, who without a doubt was the love that never wavered. If my assessment is correct, the last trip will be through Olivia's eyes.

"So, if there is only one more trip, what *is* to come after?" I ask.

"That is up to the Unbound Love to decide, isn't it?" She winks. "But sadly, some souls learn the answer when they are not ready." She turns somber, with heavy eyes. "They become discouraged by the suffering. Their heart stops beating before their soul can fully understand its gift."

"What gift?" Anthony questions.

"Silly child, are you not a gift?"

He's stalled. "I don't see how."

"Well, you are here, aren't you?" she challenges. "Do not doubt the potential of your existence, for when too many souls fall victim to grief, their pain can suppress the prosperity of others. The consequences can be devastating. Have you not caught on, dear boy? This is why the jewelry box exists. Saving one soul can save humanity."

"But that's hypothetical, right?" he questions. "Since the box exists, enough souls will be saved."

"But it *does* happen, you see. The jewelry box cannot work alone. It needs help, and when it does not get that help, the Unbound Love cannot manage the sorrow of the souls passing through. The scale will tip and a dark period will follow. The world will endure chaos before the dawn of a new renaissance. It won't last forever, but a generation's happiness may be sacrificed."

Of course, these periods in history are well researched. The Dark Ages of Europe, Imperialism, the Great Depression, World War II, the Syrian Refugee Crisis...the list goes on. It is fair to conclude: the jewelry box keeps busy.

"But we cannot forget," Meira adds, in a lighter tone, tucking a single, fallen curl behind the nook of her ear. "There is also a need for a touch of pain. Like a fire, it must be controlled. If given free reign, pain suffocates those who seek air, but in small doses, pain brings clarity to what must be changed. Pain fuels action. Pain fuels ingenuity. If we are burnt, we learn. Trust that pain will pass, and when it does, we're freshly aware of our mortality, and more appreciative of the opportunities received."

Beside me, I see Olivia grin. Her hazel eyes, no longer dulled by age, are again vibrant, preserved by curiosity. She stares at the jewelry box that started this journey and spins its base for a complete view. Together, we admire the curves and craftsmanship, and of course, the coveted opals. Her finger traces the abstract design, touching the intricate, finely cut tiles then moves onto the infinite ten-point and pentagram stars that surround it, focusing on each bump and ridge as if it were braille.

For Olivia's eighty-seventh birthday, my mom organized an outing to the Fisher Theater in Detroit's New Center neighborhood. *Spamalot* was showing, the theatrical adaptation of the film *Monty Python and the Holy Grail*, and though it wasn't her first choice, Mom felt it was most important that Olivia return to the theatre, so the tickets were purchased. It was just the three of us.

Aunt Olivia was a theatre usher for years—the Detroit Opera House, the Masonic Temple, the Fox—she worked them all, mostly because it guaranteed free entry. She spoke most highly of the Fisher and its art deco details. "Look up," she said, pointing to a mural of eagles, their wings spread with poise. "The Eagles of Zeus, who flew above the armies of Greece. They signify the potential of art, for when dedicated to higher ideals, creativity will rise above the conflicts of man."

The comedy turned out to be an unexpected hit. When the satirical chorus of knights belted their final tune, encouraging the audience to "always look on the bright side of life," my eyes were on Olivia: hands clapping and shoulders swaying, even joining in when her memory served her. Then, as the final curtain closed and the crowd rose to their feet, despite a two-week post-op hip, Olivia stood tall.

What Meira says may be true, that Olivia's third eye had closed. I can't help but think that there were moments throughout her life when it peeked, when Olivia felt the beauty of the Unbound Love. Perhaps we all have that capability, with or without the jewelry box.

Meira leans over and softly speaks to Olivia. "You've suffered greatly in this identity. The universe wishes to right its wrongs. The jewelry box found you to tip the scale to the side of good and give hope to your descendants. It summoned your third eye, the eye that was awakened within when you were shown the inner workings of the universe beyond the façade of the material world. When you became aware of what we cannot, or refuse to, see."

Meira's voice lowers to a whisper. "Dear Olivia, you were but a child, and the pain from that night stunted your growth. Soon, you had forgotten the warmth of the Unbound Love, but every now and then, it'd find you."

Again, the jewelry box pops, startling Anthony and I, but the ladies are reposed, and almost expectant. An object bangs against its interior. A new memento waits inside, the delivery for the seventh trip.

27

OLIVIA, EIGHTY-EIGHT YEARS OLD (PRESENT TIME)

The seventh trip calls.

Seven is a number revered throughout civilization. The Bible describes the seven days of creation. Hindu belief details seven chakras one must ascend, the seventh being Sahasrara, or the state of pure consciousness. Seven is the sum of three and four—three alluding to divinity, and four representing the physical earth, therefore making seven the bridge of the two realms, a gateway to transcendence. Seven colors comprise a rainbow, an emblem of peace and truce. Even Shakespeare found significance in the number, claiming man will enact seven ages in his comedy *As You Like It*, where he writes, "Last scene of all / That ends this strange eventful history / Is second childishness and mere oblivion / Sans teeth, sans eyes, sans taste, sans everything."

I have learned that after a soul tastes death, it returns starkly aware of the impermanence—and insignificance—of a physical body. Value is not attributed to financial worth, social class, or desirability, for these will not carry on. These are things that can be—and will be—left behind, for their material weight holds them back.

As for a second childishness, the gift of old age should be celebrated, for at birth and near death we are closest to the love from which we came and to which we return. If one should be so lucky as to ripen, old age is a second chance to bask in the wonder of the ever-present Unbound Love while still observing the physical world, a second chance for freedom from social constraints, when actions and expressions are uninhibited, natural.

We sit in anticipatory silence. I am comfortable in my body, accepting and embracing my familiar pudgy belly and rounded cheeks, the same features found in the eccentric, jovial Budai. My smile widens, realizing that after all these years, I finally understand why the Buddha statue that greeted me in Chinese restaurants looked so happy.

I embrace the hidden highway of light and mingle with the souls traveling the elusive dark matter that weaves amongst the living. The matter that generates awe in an admirer of the night sky, so-called empty space loaded with particles that continually form and disappear, circulating an immense amount of energy that we couldn't begin to calculate. Constantly in transit, ever changing, preparing for incoming souls to spin the wheel, and perhaps simultaneously, preparing others to bud.

I sense my father's presence, and then Sam's. Perhaps not the whole of what they once were, what I knew them to be, but an element of them. Then, like a wave of euphoria, a part of Rhona finds me in passing, making a pit stop while transcending dimensions, somehow reliving the moment of birth and reflecting on our faces, her mother and father.

As Einstein's theory of relativity suggests, the speed of time is relative to the observer, time dilation is the difference. While I was on the outskirts of the hurricane, accustomed to a slower pace, Rhona never veered far from the eye of the storm, always traveling closer to the speed of light. We were two souls in a hospital room, seemingly experiencing the same events but in our own time. What occurred in a flash for me was a lifetime for Rhona, and try as I may, I couldn't keep up.

"I'm ready." I place the third eye on the table, prepared to accept the final gift. Meira flicks the metal clasp, unhooking the latch.

"The final trip is for you, and you alone," she instructs. "Your soul was rattled at fifteen, but it was not until you were well into your sixties that your third eye fully opened."

My expression must give me away, because she stops.

"You didn't even realize it, did you? The moment it happened?"

I shake my head. She smiles.

"Nearly dying is one way to jolt your soul, the *blunt* way, but there are others. And, sometimes, we mustn't do anything at all. The Unbound Love wishes you peace, the peace you once found, and now, it will remind you."

The jewelry box opens. Meira lifts a Polaroid photograph from its cubby. Immediately, I remember the moment, and for the first time since the jewelry box arrived, I am eager for the trip.

June clasps my arm. Anthony completes the circle by holding the free hands of the women beside him. Meira hovers the photograph above my palm's eye, and as it makes contact, I'm transported into the moment, when for once in my life, the world felt right.

28

OLIVIA, SIXTY-SEVEN YEARS OLD (TWENTY-ONE YEARS AGO)

Not sure what in God's name possessed my niece and nephew to plan a trip to Yellowstone National Park in August. I've lost a pint of blood to man-eating mosquitoes and was likely gifted malaria in exchange for my generous donation.

Every summer Jack and Linda take a family vacation, and every summer they ask me to join. This year, I finally agreed.

It's the first trip since Dottie passed. Linda hasn't mentioned her mom, but she's on her mind, I can tell. She's on mine, too. After being diagnosed with dementia—or as Dr. Cullin described it, "Alzheimer's, but worse"—Dottie lived three years, and then, at age sixty-five, succumbed to the illness. To be frank, it was a blessing. She began acting bizarrely—stealing the tip money before leaving a restaurant, lashing out when Linda purchased the wrong brand of cereal—and, according to the statistics, was high risk for Lou Gehrig's disease, a killer in its own right.

Then there's me, same ol' Aunt Olivia who's still here. I know how they view me—a lonely old woman with no family of her own. But I don't need pity. What they, and the world, don't realize is I am more than capable of filling my time. Still, I appreciate the gesture. I enjoy being with June. I've had an affinity for her since the day she was born. She has spirit. How I imagined Rhona would be.

Jack found a deal on two authentic, rustic cabins in the northern end of the park. Our porch overlooks Lamar Valley, what the brochure describes as America's Serengeti. The land seems pleasant, with elk roaming free and osprey overhead, but when the park ranger warned that neglected banana peels attract grizzly bears, I slept with one eye open, almost peeing the bed when a long-tailed weasel assaulted a camping chair.

"Dad!" June's gnawing the cuff of her oversized sweatshirt, arms tightly folded to trap heat. The mornings are chilled, even during the hottest and muggiest month of the year. She stands at the edge of our site, looking onto the prairie over a row of tree tops.

"Come quickly," she urges. I stand to see what the fuss is about. Jack, in the middle of assembling hobo pies, sprints to her side.

He sighs, relieved. "Beautiful, aren't they? Those are bison, baby doll. The pride of the grasslands." Jack's beaming. It's as if he's waited his entire life to say that, channeling his best John Wayne.

From here, they resemble ants. I grab my binoculars. There are six in total, five full grown and one calf, half the size of his elders. The adults circle him as he feeds, a fortress of muscle and fur. A majestic animal with a bipolar personality, ready to rage when threatened and kill when it's their babies at risk. Jack wraps his arm around June. Though the herd is a good three to four miles away, he also has the need to protect his young.

"Ready, Ol?" Linda joins me on the porch swing, which creaks with the added weight. "We have a nature walk today," she declares, overly perky before eight in the morning She takes sips of steaming coffee from her brand-new Yellowstone National Park mug, embellished with the silhouette of a black bear against a backdrop of pine trees.

I nod with a sleep-deprived smile. "Ready whenever." I read the detailed Excel spreadsheet handed to me the morning we embarked for the park. Linda's a planner. Not my style, but I roll with it.

Jack and Linda load the car. "Pile in," he yells, holding the door and waving me in with the rigid, precise movements of a crossing guard. June and I share the back seat. She takes her half-eaten breakfast to go, and with it the aroma of charcoal-broiled, seasoned potatoes and melted cheese. A drifter's hash.

The lodge is maybe five miles from our cabin, if that, but the landscape becomes vastly different, depressingly so. Moments ago we were surrounded by sprawling green forest. Now it looks like a wasteland. *The Twilight Zone* twist disturbs me. Green foliage sprouts between the charred, dead trees, but the neglect of the land is unbefitting, even lazy. The tree graveyard mars the tranquil vista.

Jack turns onto a gravel road, and loose stones pop like gunshots against the car door. Linda cringes, anticipating the chipped paint job she'll find when we park.

A young ranger greets us under a driftwood arch. He looks about fifteen but he's probably in college, earning credits in the field rather than stuck inside a stuffy classroom. We're the first group of the day. He rubs his hands with excitement and enough friction to spark a flame. Eager to begin, his cracking voice calls us into line: "Gather round!"

Jack stands at attention, hands by his side, while Linda takes notes. She records locations and dates so photographs can be labeled after she develops the film. It's her hobby and passion, diligently archiving family milestones from behind a lens.

Then there's June, my kind of traveler. A child who requires amusement and isn't eager to please. "Why's this area such a dump?"

"June Edith!" Appalled, Linda snaps her notebook shut.

"Well, ah." The ranger's taken aback. I let a chuckle slip. He dives into his prepared speech. "The land endured the fire of 1988. Wildfires have helped the dynamics of Yellowstone's ecosystem for hundreds of years, but about six years ago, this place turned into an inferno when over seven thousand acres were torched in a devastating fire that lasted months..."

Linda tugs June's sleeve, ensuring that she will listen to the explanation if she was to so rudely ask the question. But I have the luxury of not caring, so I let his voice trail off. In its place, a chorus of songbirds and waterfowl, a much more pleasant, peaceful sound: nature's symphony. My mind wanders.

A split second later, my sneaker snags a wayward root, and I tumble, head first, into what looks like a telephone pole. My fractured binoculars skid down the rocky trail. The crash—or my scream—stops the tour.

"Careful now!" The ranger hustles to kneel by my side, scrambling for the first aid kit strung from his utility belt. "The *Pinus contortas* will get ya." He snickers, pointing to the tall hunk of wood whose identity I mistook.

"The penis what?" I retort. Linda covers June's ears.

"No, ah..." He blushes and reconsiders his choice of words. "It's the official species name for the lodgepole pine."

I pluck a blackened pine cone off my shin. The prickly ridges broke skin, leaving tiny, red markings. I toss it aside.

"Tough stuff, right?" He wraps an ACE bandage around my ankle, an overblown treatment for the severity of the injury. The kit looks untouched, the Band-Aids are still sealed. He's waited all summer to show off his skills.

"Don't let the burnt appearance fool you," he continues, proving he can guide a tour while saving my life. "That cone is teeming with the potential for growth. It's called serotinous."

Jack approaches. "You okay, Ol?"

"Never better," I impulsively, rather sarcastically retort. But I instantly regret it. Jack's lengthened face gives away his worry. I am the guest on this trip. It would be more becoming if I showed a little gratitude. I compensate for my saltiness by engaging the ranger. "The cone looks dead. Why's it so special to be sero...ah...ser."

"Serotinous," he corrects.

"Yeah. That."

Delighted, he retrieves the discarded cone. "Until they are subjected to temperatures of 45 to 50 degrees Celsius, the seal will not break open and the seed cannot release. Therefore, heat from a fire actually makes reproduction possible."

"I'll be damned." Normally trapped in a cubicle, Jack is fully engaged. In fact, I'd say enthralled, as if he's seeing an alternative version of himself, or what he could have been, in this scrawny young buck.

"The vegetation in Yellowstone has adapted to fire, and in some cases depends on it," the ranger continues. "By removing the forest overstory and allowing different plant communities to establish, fire promotes a diverse, thriving habitat. It's a shame you're seeing it during its rebuilding phase, but future generations will enjoy the fruits of the labor. Gives you a new appreciation for the ground those feet of yours trample over, eh?"

The ploy worked. Jack and the ranger are engaged in conversation, intently observing whatever hinterland creature scurries across the land or soars across the sky, and I'm left alone.

June stops and takes my elbow. "Need help?"

I smile, but politely decline. "Nah, I'm not hurt. Go on. I'll catch up."

She jogs to Linda, whose Nikon camera points and clicks as fast as she can focus.

Now a few steps behind, aside from the snap, crackle, and pop of the fallen branches, I walk in silence. I need a moment. These people are my family, my identified tribe, but I'm my own person. Always have been. Whether by choice or circumstance, I return to my solitude. I've grown comfortable there. Grief brings resilience, and though lonely at times, it is when I'm alone that I feel the most connected.

Once again, I hear the chorus, and now, more conscious of my surroundings, the scenery transforms.

I see the hollow, dead tree limbs as nesting cavities for animals. The decaying bark becomes the active breakdown of life-giving nutrients to the soil, the living and the dead coexisting, one feeding into the other. The impairment is not the forest, it's my expectation for what I deem to be beautiful and, more so, my impatience.

I spot June. They're gathered at a lookout area along the trail. It sits on a hill with views of the valley below, a Petri dish of vegetation. Patches of the lodgepole pine stick straight from the earth like a giant's used toothpicks. I rejoin them, but stay toward the back.

"Those are the burned lodgepole pines. The parents to that cone," the ranger informs them. "They can take a hundred years to reach maturity and can live as long as a hundred and forty years."

It seems senseless. Sad, really. After one hundred years of growth, they're ravaged by fire and stripped of the needles that brightened their branches, gone just like that.

Our ranger stops at the sound of incoming chatter. Another group joins us, much to his annoyance. They started later, but our breaks have delayed our progress. The August heat is building. The rangers strike up a conversation to allow time to rest.

Linda seizes the opportunity for taking photographs, this time with her Polaroid, purchased specifically for the trip. I find a stump next to June and Jack, who share a bag of trail mix. They don't notice me grunt as I squat. They're mid-conversation, June's gangly legs dangling from her father's lap.

"You can't rush the process," Jack tells his daughter, nudging her with his canteen and hinting she take a sip. He speaks of the forest.

"How long will it take to rebuild?" she asks, innocence in her voice. To a nine-year-old, minutes last forever, and days are an eternity.

"As long as it needs to." He strings the canteen through his belt loop. "You heard the ranger, maybe another hundred and forty years."

June's mouth drops as she does the math. "That means I won't get to see it." She pouts, heartbroken.

Jack pulls her close, digging his chin into the hair of her ponytail. "Instant gratification is tempting," he begins, but then pauses. His face lights up.

He balances June while shifting through his pocket. "Don't tell the ranger." He winks, and presents the offending pinecone while checking to ensure the ranger's still preoccupied. "We're not supposed to take souvenirs that weren't purchased at the gift shop."

He drags his fingers down the seeds like the ridges of a washboard. "If gratification came at the snap of our fingers it would cheapen the work ethic of the fallen seeds. They have the promise of being as grandiose as their parents. They're just begging for the time to do it." He spins the cone on June's palm. "This little guy's fascinating. It must travel through hell and back before blossoming. A true phoenix."

Confused, she asks, "Like the city?"

He can't help but chuckle. "No, honey. A phoenix is a Greek mythical bird. When a phoenix dies in a fiery blaze, a new life sparks by rising from its ashes. As they say, 'ashes to ashes.' Our bodies are impermanent, fragile. Like the forest, in the blink of an eye it could go *poof*!" His flailed arms exaggerate an explosion.

June giggles and falls back, her ponytail dusting the dirt. It's a touching moment between a child and a parent. I stay quiet, continuing to listen.

His voice turns somber. "Baby girl." His hairy arms swipe the sweat brought on by the midday sun. "Nothing is forever—the forests, the pine cones, even me. It's OK to want to feel safe. Security isn't a bad thing. You need it in *some* aspect of your life to keep you grounded when another aspect unravels, but don't be naïve to its vulnerability. Everything must change, and it will do it when it needs to, whether you're ready or not."

He tosses the pine cone onto the earth, not back into his pocket where it was a stowaway. It nestles comfortably in the nourishing dirt. He rocks her gently. "What I strive for, and what I wish for you, is to successfully disperse the love and generosity we were meant to share, in the time we've been given to do it."

She nods, clinging to her dad's every word. I question if she comprehends their weight, but I pray she does. I hope she remembers this forever. I will.

"Take your Aunt Ol, for example," he adds.

I nearly choke on air, terrified of what I'm about to hear. What do I possibly have to do with this?

"If you're one of the fortunate ones, you'll be like her. She found her greatest security within herself. Her life was tossed on its head at a very young age. Ask her about it sometime. But she rallied and built the safest sanctuary of all, and it's given her great freedom."

June looks to her dad in thought, her ears absorbing his words.

"Cheese!" Linda surprises us. The flash temporarily blinds me. "An action shot. My favorite."

The print spits out of the camera's slot. She gives it a shake to rush the development. "Here ya go, Ol." She smiles and presents the gift.

"Mom! Look," June yells. Her eyes and nose wrinkle, her tongue sticks straight out. She's an experienced subject, Linda's favorite, hamming it up for the camera.

"Work it, baby girl!" Linda jokes, rapidly capturing the image. Jack joins in, contorting his face for a laugh.

As I hold the photo, the white disappears and an image takes shape. Colors pop out of thin air while arms and legs form definition. It depicts the three of us perched on our respective stumps. The exuberance in June's smile has her neck muscles tensed, while Jack's is soft, with a glimmer of pride. Behind us a celestial sky, balanced by the earthy greens and browns of the budding forest.

A peace comes over me with the realization that this perfect moment has passed. I take another glance, admiring the faces of those I love, and then place the photograph in my purse. There's a tightness in my chest, not from sorrow, but from gratitude. Gratitude for Jack's words and his willingness to see the good in me, for the kindness in the souls that the universe chose to surround me with, and for Mother Nature, the true teacher, who has the answers to our questions if we take time to listen.

I breathe in and taste a new moment, letting go of what has passed and premonitions of what's to come. Right now, all is right.

I am grateful.

"One more group shot!" Linda calls, waving me into the frame.

"Hold on," I protest. "You need to be in this one." I whistle for our ranger's assistance. The four of us squeeze in tight.

"One, two, and—" The ranger takes the photo on three. The flash of the camera's bulb causes an array of colors to shimmy down my body, crawling to the tips of my fingers and toes and returning to my heart.

My soul is captured, taken from my body, now hovering above. Once again, I feel the presence of the light—the Unbound Love—but this time, there's no going back.

With deep appreciation, I thank my body and say farewell to the life it gave me; the good, the bad, and all that falls in between. For without fire, the seed will not grow.

29

ANTHONY, TWENTY-EIGHT YEARS OLD (PRESENT TIME)

She's gone.

Olivia's rigid muscles hold their shape like clay left to dry. Her expression is set in stone. Her eyes are fixed on the object before her—me—but refuse to blink. Her eyes lack dimension, and though I duck and weave, they relentlessly track me like those of a portrait painting.

June sucks in snot. Her sweater sleeve is soaked with fallen tears. She knows. We all know. Olivia's soul veered. She's *gone*.

Meira tenderly embraces the body. She closes the lids of Olivia's eyes with the tips of her thumbs. It's a relief. Meira speaks of death so freely, has no qualms about hugging a corpse, and though I can accept what we've learned, I still want nothing to do with it. That's not Olivia, it's a slowly decomposing hunk of tissue. Unable to bear it, I turn away.

Meira spreads her fingers and clamps Olivia's skull. She swirls her hair, messing the familiar slicked-back, low ponytail, then pushes her own third eye into the spot between Olivia's brows.

"Her body still has memory," she reports. "Her soul hasn't made it far, but she's traveling fast. She's very independent, no? Her soul's resistant to losing its physical form."

"Sounds about right." June laughs through tears. "Did you know this would happen?"

Meira licks her fingertips to smooth back Olivia's mangled hair. "It was possible," she admits.

"Why didn't you warn us?" June's tone rises. "We could have said goodbye!"

Meira shakes her head. "Sweet June, do not worry about Olivia. Though you may not be ready, she was." She's candid without commiseration.

With a deep breath, June holds it together, barely. Her red face and trembling jaw are like a teapot suppressing steam. Meira unties and offers her canary yellow scarf. "There, there. Now blow into this, dear."

June accepts and doesn't hold back. With a forceful blow, the delicate fabric is soiled. She offers it back, but Meira politely declines. "You can have that, dear. It's on me."

Meira then selects an apricot cookie and places it outside the circumference of the plate, directly on the table's surface, an uncharacteristic move that opposes her immaculate, hygienic nature. "June, tell me about the Earth and the moon."

"I, ah, I'm not sure what you want to know."

"Here. Let me help," she insists, readying her props. "The moon orbits the Earth because of gravity. As the Earth spins, the fabric of space that surrounds it shifts. This creates a dent. The moon continually slides into that dent, pulled along the curvature of the Earth until it eventually comes full circle, then does it again."

She slowly mimics this notion. The cookie is the moon, and the plate is the Earth. The cookie trails the plate's rotation until it completes a full revolution around the circumference.

"This goes on for as long as they are tied by proximity," she continues. "Lucky for the moon, it has a guide, but in this relationship, the moon is also overshadowed. We see this when it waxes and wanes." She sets the objects aside and faces June. "Remember, dear, that the closest object in orbit is flung the hardest when its primary implodes. You have a choice. You must find a different, larger object to orbit or grow large enough to attract them *to you*."

June nods, and then leans over to kiss Olivia's cheek. She envelops her great-aunt's hands with hers. She clenches her eyes shut and under her breath mumbles a prayer, saying her goodbyes.

I'll miss Olivia, sure, but it's not because of her. It's because of June.

It's realizing that I was the last reason June cried, and I can deny it all I want, but the pain I caused has impacted her health, and the proof is in the way her ribs now protrude through her cotton t-shirt. It's admitting, finally, that I knew June would take me in when I knocked on her door this morning. I knew that it could set her back emotionally, but I didn't care, because she wasn't my concern. I was. If Meira has so many answers, can she please explain why I hurt those closest to me?

Yet, despite feeling unworthy, here I am.

Outside of these four walls is an abandoned lot surrounded by a graveyard of automotive frames, a landmine to solicitors that says *Do Not Disturb*. We are secluded, the oyster protecting the pearl, the keepers of a secret that could change the world—if anyone would believe us—but I have to ask, do *I* believe it?

"It's vanished!" June shouts, showing Olivia's palm.

Olivia's third eye has disappeared. Her palms are delicate, pruney soft to the touch and no more extraordinary than any other that belong to a woman her age.

Meira nods. "Its job is done."

Meira treats the body like an artifact. "There." She plucks a loose thread from Olivia's collar, and with two swift taps, perfectly straightens the shoulder's hem. It's remarkable how a properly fitted garment improves an appearance. For once, Olivia's blouse is not consumed by the underside of her boobs. Meira pins the sunflower pendant onto her blouse atop her static heart. The finishing touch.

She sits back to admire her work.

"How do you know all of this?" I ask.

"I learned from the best." Coyly, the corners of her red lips curl upward. "My mother was a master of the craft. She could sense when souls crossed years before the jewelry box found them. It's how she found Olivia, and it's how she met my father, though I don't recommend falling in love with your conquest. What a drag, always living in paranoia. If the post office delivered a package, she treated it like a bomb."

"Wait, what?" June catches the subtle slip. "Olivia met your mother?"

"Certainly, but Olivia wouldn't have known," she confirms, delighted to share details. "It was my mother who first sensed Olivia's soul had veered and sought her at the funeral days after. My mother's keen sense gave her an advantage, but if a soul's crossing was tragic, it also posed a dilemma," she explains. "The jewelry box can take years, often decades, to find its chosen beneficiary. She quite rightfully sensed young Olivia was troubled by the accident, and she always had a special affinity for her soul. She wished the pendant would give Olivia hope until the jewelry box could bring her peace. It's pure sterling silver. The most *exquisite* craftsmanship."

The polished ridges of the sunflower's petals somehow manage to sparkle in the dimmed room.

"Once the jewelry box is delivered, it tends to work quickly, but in Olivia's case it was dormant for years. I've been patient, but I must admit, Olivia was my toughest conquest yet. For the first time in my life I dove through trash. It was quite unbecoming."

Suddenly, it hits me. *Of course*. The crazy lady James described, it was Meira.

She struts toward the window in a dramatic fashion, arms extended with her chest leading. "I thought I'd miscalculated its arrival, but after meeting you both, I believe this mission is most unique and extends beyond Olivia."

She grasps the cloth of the hanging curtains. "Shut your eyes. What do you notice?"

Anxious, June looks to me. I shut mine first, letting her know we have nothing to lose.

Without sight, other senses push forward. I smell the musk of tobacco absorbed into old walls and the stale air from grimy, neglected ductwork. I feel a bent cross rail on the dilapidated, wooden dining room chair poke and prod my spine. Then, there's a sense I can't define. Periodically, bursts of euphoria rise from my tailbone to the top of my skull. Twice, then three times. I smile.

Meira whips open the curtains. The sun's rays spill into the room. The abrupt change in lighting forces my eyes open, and once my vision adjusts, I find June smiling, too.

Meira stands before us, statuesque. Light floods over and blurs the outline of her body, creating a mystical silhouette framed by the window's trim.

"Wonderful, isn't it?" she asks. "Those are souls crossing."

She spins around with a ballerina's grace, then lets her arms flop. Her perfect posture droops. For once, she allows herself to relax.

"I'm tired," she confesses. "But thankfully you two are here to carry on my work."

"Excuse me?" June's wide eyes speak for both of us.

"Your ignorance is gone," Meira soberly points out. "From now on, you exist at the crossroads, one foot in this realm and one in the next. The Unbound Love appoints tagalongs and beneficiaries. You two were accomplices on Olivia's journey and will now go on to live as tagalongs, just as I did. Though you'll need a new pager." She glowers, and then airily chuckles. "I suppose that component could be updated."

She extends her arms and admires their shape, twirling and looping her wrists. "But, as you can imagine, this knowledge does have its downsides. I miss myself before I'm gone. I quite like this identity."

Immediately, I flip over my hands. Nothing's there. No eye or odd growth of any kind. "Will we get one of *those?*" I point to the third eye on her palm.

"If you're lucky." She winks and stands a little taller. "It's very rare for a tagalong. You must embark on many trips. I'm permanently aware of traveling souls, so my third eye stays open. It's always protected."

"But what if we don't want to do this?" It's a bold, impulsive counter, but I have my own shit to deal with. I'm far from equipped to guide others.

Her brow furrows, accentuating an austere, no-bullshit stare. Her high heels tap-dance across the hardwood. She hovers at my feet.

"I cannot force you to accept your fate. Though he had potential, Lenny chose to renounce the responsibility. It wasn't for him, and I quite respect that. He had his own journey in mind. But it was a different time then. Recently, I sense the scale has tilted, and not in the favor of what is good. Lenny understands this, too. It's why he helps when he can."

"You don't seem much older than Lenny. Why did you say yes?" I ask.

She bends at the waist, leaning closer. "I told you my father was a beneficiary, like Olivia. Would you like to know why?"

I nod.

"My father had the great misfortune of being a young Jewish boy in Germany. The Nazis took him to Auschwitz, a death camp, and it was there, locked in a pitch-black chamber in Block 11, that he felt the Unbound Love. He lived a long life—much thanks due to my mother—but he carried the hurt of that experience. Finally, the jewelry box arrived on his eighty-second birthday."

She returns to the bookshelf and grazes the bindings until she finds the one of interest. From it, she steals an object, a bookmark entombed between the first page and the cover's flap. It's a tattered badge, golden in hue in the shape of a six-point star. The word *Jude* is stitched in its center. "His first gift."

She balances the derogatory emblem on her breast.

"Please, Anthony. The hateful actions and rhetoric that plagued my father's generation is a testament to what can happen when the Unbound Love is overwhelmed by pain. A beneficiary's pain—Olivia's pain—is yours, and it is mine. It bleeds into the Unbound Love, the same loves that feed us all. We must do all we can to tip the scale to good. We must affirm the troubled souls."

Before I can respond, her hand is in my pocket. She pinches the newspaper clipping and dangles it in front of my eyes. My father's image stares me down, challenging my reluctance.

"Anthony, your father never learned his worth, and because of it, you suffered, too. Please, though he has passed, find his body. Maybe one day he'll revisit this identity. Maybe he'll find his peace." With a light toss, she floats the obituary onto my lap.

Though the photo is pixelated with poor resolution, it is clear that from his eyes came my own. I am a part of him.

We all are.

Beside me, June comforts Winston, or vice versa, but regardless, I am not the one she needs. If we are to take on the role of a tagalong that Meira described, we are to do it separately, breaking our codependence. We are two planets, sharing the same solar system, attracting our own moons.

With a flick of Meira's wrist, two pennies appear. After inspecting the coins for grime, she licks the copper, using spit as an adhesive, and then rests them atop Olivia's eyelids. It's a custom I've witnessed in films but never in person.

"A Greek tradition," she explains, "to pay the fare when she crosses the river to the afterlife." She lifts Olivia's chin to keep the coins balanced. "But I like to think pennies *for* heaven become pennies *from* heaven. Tiny tokens that sneak into a new dimension and defy the laws of physics." She bows her head and then places her lips against Olivia's ear, whispering a farewell: "*Shalom*."

EPILOGUE: JUNE, TWENTY-EIGHT YEARS OLD (PRESENT TIME)

The familiar bell rings as I walk into Café Ardenne. The weekday atmosphere is calm, a far cry from the busy Sunday crowd of our last visit.

This morning we laid Olivia to rest. Well, her body at least. Exactly one week and one day since her death. While driving Meira home, I remembered Jacoby's advice: *find the sacredness*. I returned to the café for inspiration, and even if my expectations fall flat, at least I'll be soothed with a latte.

Anthony contacted the Wayne County Medical Examiner's office last Monday morning, and so did I. My mother was insistent that a cause of death be determined, tormented that she was at fault, neglectful of her aunt's needs. As expected, it returned without suspicion of foul play. Olivia's heart simply stopped.

My unemployment allowed the time to plan funeral arrangements. We opted to have Olivia cremated. It was her wish, despite the urging of the priest to respect the interment of the body. "He can respect it as dust," her estate attorney quoted her saying, and thanks to her detailed notes referencing the 1983 revision of the Catholic Church's *Code of Canon Law*, she couldn't be argued against.

Olivia's service was held at Ste. Anne de Detroit before half-filled pews. It was modest, mostly close family and friends, with a few second cousins she'd periodically seen at holidays or weddings. Most of her childhood friends have passed, and from what we could tell, she kept to herself in the nursing home.

The church was the location of Olivia's christening more than eighty years ago. The two steeples, book-ending the Gothic Revival entrance, stood tall when the urn was carried up the steps through the gargoyles, who welcomed her back with open arms. In the forefront of the cityscape was the Ambassador Bridge, an industrial reminder of the proximity of the Detroit River. *Don't forget your pennies,* I thought.

The ceremonial mass adhered to Catholic tradition—Introduction Rites, Liturgy of the Word, and the Final Commendation—but in true Meira style, last minute instructions were given for a special addition. The priest approached me as the death knell rang. "Excuse me, miss." Tapping my shoulder to deliver a crinkled piece of notebook paper. "She wanted you to read this." He pointed to the woman sitting front row, dolled up in a floral pantsuit with a peacock-feathered fascinator atop her nest of curls. An odd choice for a somber occasion.

Scrawled in the top margin, it read: *A letter from Einstein on the death of his good friend, Michele Besso*. Below that, with no regard to the ruled paper's lines, was a handwritten quote:

Now he has departed from this strange world a little ahead of me. That signifies nothing. For those of us who believe in physics, the distinction between past, present, and future is only a stubbornly persistent illusion.

I read it, word for word, as confused eyes peered from the pews. Few understood the reference, but it needn't matter. They instead found peace in the other, familiar teachings: *Brothers and sisters, hope does not disappoint. We have a building from God, eternal in heaven.*

After Olivia's ceremony, Anthony planned to spread Robert's ashes over the Detroit River from Belle Isle—where Aunt Elaine told of Labor Day barbeques spent playing Michigan rummy and euchre, and of a much happier Robert. When we spoke, he mentioned winning a thousand dollars on a lotto ticket, which he used to buy cremation services and an urn. I was happy for him. He deserves a stroke of luck.

I asked if he wanted company, but after some consideration, he thought it'd be best to go alone. He mentioned needing space, and deep down, I was relieved. What our roles will be in each other's lives is uncertain, and safe to say, forever changed. But I've been surprised before. Perhaps he'll show up at my door again announced, making a wisecrack about my coffee. If he does, my instincts tell me it will be a while. For both of us, it's for the best.

So many questions are left since Aunt Olivia's passing. Our hypothesis is just that, a *hypothesis,* and there's no shortage of takers to reject, nullify, or disprove what Meira suggests. Is this identity impermanent? Meira seems to think so, but there are others who are equally as certain of a proper afterlife—heaven, with harps, and relatives, and God presiding over the grand party, welcoming home his guests at the pearly gates with a red wine toast.

Then again, maybe the mystics are correct—the practices of Tasawwuf, Kabbalah, and the lesser acknowledged elements of Christian theology—those that celebrate the extraordinary within the ordinary by embracing divinity's omnipresence. Or maybe the Gnostics, who feel grace lies within, it's the energy that sustains. Or the Evangelicals, who regard biblical authority and await a heaven that far exceeds the life this Earth provides. Or maybe the rational scientists who study neurology and conclude that we are merely a hunk of matter—a hundred billion reactive neurons continually transmitting signals that one day *stop*.

I don't know what I believe or if I'll ever find a concrete answer, but I can't deny what I feel, and when I sense the warmth of the souls crossing I believe there is more to this universe. And that, regardless of the prayers a soul chooses to speak while encased in a body, once released, there's an equal opportunity to break the speed of light and contribute to the Unbound Love.

While we're here, in bodies weighted by gravity, we have no input as to what our earthly eyes will see. We *must* see it all, and we *must* accept it all. We only control how we will react. Now, after experiencing the power of the opals and with Olivia gone, I must decide, how will I?

The café counter's abandoned. Snatching the closest chair, I twirl a strand of hair, then wince when it snaps, snagged by my wedding ring. I take a long, good look, and for the first time since saying our vows, slide it off my finger and into my purse pocket.

"Welcome back!" a deep voice calls. I'm the only patron here.

It's the barista, returning from the stockroom. He wears a different version of what must be his signature plaid. His hair is still untamed, in a good way. He fills the empty chair beside me, then leans onto elbows stained with ground coffee beans. There's an optimism about him that's contagious.

"Can I share some good news?" he asks.

"Of course." I nod, returning his smile.

"I was hoping you'd say that." He puts me at ease. "I just got off the phone with my sister. She had her baby yesterday, and after a long night of complications, the doctors took my niece off life support. She's stabilized and breathing on her own. I'm an uncle to a seven-pound, two-ounce baby girl!" He proudly shows a photo saved on his cell phone. A woman cradles an infant. A tiny tube plugs the child's nose, yet she's serene, secure in her mother's arms. A full head of thick, wavy hair peaks through her blue and pink striped hat. "They decided on Mae." He beams. "I think it has a nice ring to it."

"It sure does," I confirm. "Short and sweet."

"This calls for a celebration." He peruses the glass case of muffins. After deciding on banana walnut, he places a plate between us and slices evenly down the middle, offering me half. Without reservation, he devours the cake. Turbinado sugar frosts his beard. I envy his lack of inhibition.

"Thanks," I mutter, picking at a fallen crumb.

Then, an unusually strong, blissful sensation—a passing soul—stimulates my nerves, and I recall Meira's words, "From now on, you exist at the crossroads, one foot in this realm and one in the next." Though apprehensive of the work I have before me, I also acknowledge how far I've come.

"Cheers." In jest, I raise my portion and take a hardy bite. He laughs, then, using his thumb, clears the sugar from my cheek.

The Unbound Love may govern the grand scale of souls crossing over, but there is also a delicate, more pertinent balance of love and pain among the living that's entrusted to each of us: the balance between a single soul and the identity in which it coincides. Though my soul may have its own agenda when my beating heart stops, right now I am its keeper, and the responsibility to help tip this scale to the side of love is *mine*.

ACKNOWLEDGMENTS

To my daughter, Myla, my purpose: I ignorantly thought this novel's completion would be the highlight of my year, but then the universe brought you. May you rejoice in all this beautiful, messy world has to offer. I love you, my girl.

To my husband, Bryan: for your patience and willingness to endure my incessant deliberating of articles and podcasts, I thank you. I love you more than words, and as you know, I *love* words.

To my siblings by blood and choice, Dan, Andrew, Melissa and Jenny: for your inspiring fortitude and integrity. You are, and always have been, true role models.

To my parents: you've raised me to question everything, seek truth, and fiercely pursue what brings joy. It is I who hit the "jackpot," and I will forever be grateful.

To my editors, Alex Kourvo, Nichole Christian, and Amy Sumerton: your collective wisdom and attention to detail were invaluable assets. Without you, this novel would still be a mish-mash of random thoughts without a plot.

To the Ann Arbor Library's Fifth Avenue Press, especially Erin

Helmrich, Josh Barnhart, and Nathaniel Roy: thank you for giving new author's a chance, sharing your artistic skills, and responding to my countless emails. Our community is lucky to have you.

And to Charlie Jane: your love was brief, but immense, and now dispersed to us all. You are remembered.

ABOUT THE AUTHOR

Bethany Grey is an author and dietitian living in Ann Arbor, Michigan. Her passion for storytelling began with her Grandmother and matured during college, after life experience amplified the relatability of a good coming-of-age narrative.

She is a graduate of Michigan State University and earned a Master of Nutrition from Case Western Reserve University. Her articles are published in Food & Nutrition Magazine.

Her mystical family-saga, *All That We Encounter*, appeases her affinity for strong matriarchs and spiritual quests. This is her debut novel.

CPSIA information can be obtained
at www.ICGtesting.com
Printed in the USA
LVHW091745061119
636549LV00006B/1122/P